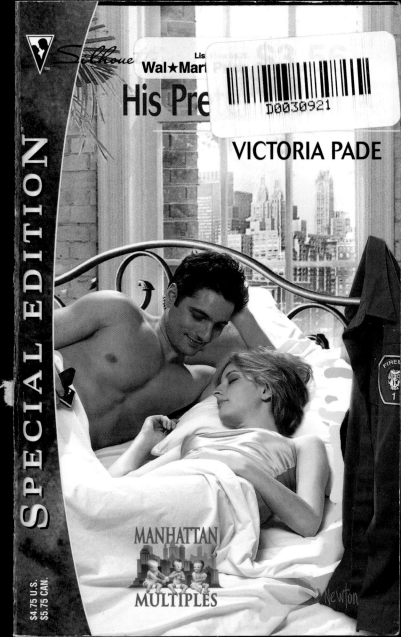

Silhouette

Wal★Mart

His Pre...

VICTORIA PADE

D0030921

SPECIAL EDITION

MANHATTAN

MULTIPLES

Newton

$4.75 U.S.
$5.75 CAN.

Silhouette®

Desire®

New York Times bestselling author

DIANA PALMER

MAN IN CONTROL

(Silhouette Desire #1537)

A brand-new

LONG, TALL
Texans
title.

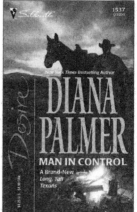

ISBN 0-373-24564-2

9 780373 245642

5 0 4 7 5

Eight years ago, DEA agent Alexander Cobb gave Jodie Clayburn a Texas-size brush-off. Now a covert investigation is making allies out of sworn enemies. When peril follows them home, can they remain in control? Tantalized to the core, this *Long, Tall Texan* would risk anything to protect—and possess— the woman he just can't resist.

*Available October 2003
at your favorite retail outlet.*

⊲ EAN

Dear Reader,

Breeze into fall with six rejuvenating romances from Silhouette Special Edition! We are happy to feature our READERS' RING selection, *Hard Choices* (SE#1561), by favorite author Allison Leigh, who writes, "I wondered about the masks people wear, such as the 'good' girl/boy vs. the 'bad' girl/boy, and what ultimately hardens or loosens those masks. Annie and Logan have worn masks that don't fit, and their past actions wouldn't be considered ideal behavior. I hope readers agree this is a thought-provoking scenario!"

We can't get enough of Pamela Toth's WINCHESTER BRIDES miniseries as she delivers the next book, *A Winchester Homecoming* (SE#1562). Here, a world-weary heroine comes home only to find her former flame ready to reignite their passion. MONTANA MAVERICKS: THE KINGSLEYS returns with Judy Duarte's latest, *Big Sky Baby* (SE#1563). In this tale, a Kingsley cousin comes home to find that his best friend is pregnant. All of a sudden, he can't stop thinking of starting a family…with her!

Victoria Pade brings us an engagement of convenience and a passion of *in*convenience, in *His Pretend Fiancée* (SE#1564), the next book in the MANHATTAN MULTIPLES miniseries. Don't miss *The Bride Wore Blue Jeans* (SE#1565), the last in veteran Marie Ferrarella's miniseries, THE ALASKANS. In this heartwarming love story, a confirmed bachelor flies to Alaska and immediately falls for the woman least likely to marry! In *Four Days, Five Nights* (SE#1566) by Christine Flynn, two strangers are forced to face a growing attraction when their small plane crashes in the wilds.

These moving romances will foster discussion, escape and lots of daydreaming. Watch for more heart-thumping stories that show the joys and complexities of a woman's world.

Happy reading!

Karen Taylor Richman,
Senior Editor

Please address questions and book requests to:
Silhouette Reader Service
U.S.: 3010 Walden Ave., P.O. Box 1325, Buffalo, NY 14269
Canadian: P.O. Box 609, Fort Erie, Ont. L2A 5X3

"I have a crazy idea." *Michael Dunnigan smiled.*

"My mother will never stop matchmaking until she believes I've found someone," he added.

And that made him think of me? A hopeful little flutter in the pit of her stomach gave Josie pause.

"Well, since you need a place to stay, well, I thought, what if I sort of hire you to move in with me and pretend to be my fiancée."

That made Josie laugh. "You want me to move in with you?"

"On a purely platonic basis." He smiled sheepishly again and she wished he would stop it. Smiling only made him more attractive.

Was she actually considering this?

"It's a crazy idea. But I thought crazy ideas were right up your alley," he commented.

"I don't think it would be very wise," she said suddenly. Sparks had already flown between them. It was a combustible attraction. An uncontrollable attraction.

"What if we make a pact just to be roommates, friends—"

"Coconspirators," Josie confirmed.

His Pretend Fiancée

VICTORIA PADE

Silhouette®

SPECIAL EDITION™

Published by Silhouette Books

America's Publisher of Contemporary Romance

If you purchased this book without a cover you should be aware that this book is stolen property. It was reported as "unsold and destroyed" to the publisher, and neither the author nor the publisher has received any payment for this "stripped book."

With acknowledgment and appreciation of Erin Negri for her poem "Contribution." Thank you, Erin, for the use of your work. Thanks, too, for your brilliance, wisdom and wit. I love you and I'm more proud of you than you'll ever know.

Special thanks and acknowledgment are given to Victoria Pade for her contribution to the MANHATTAN MULTIPLES series.

 SILHOUETTE BOOKS

ISBN 0-373-24564-5

HIS PRETEND FIANCÉE

Copyright © 2003 by Harlequin Books S.A.

All rights reserved. Except for use in any review, the reproduction or utilization of this work in whole or in part in any form by any electronic, mechanical or other means, now known or hereafter invented, including xerography, photocopying and recording, or in any information storage or retrieval system, is forbidden without the written permission of the editorial office, Silhouette Books, 233 Broadway, New York, NY 10279 U.S.A.

All characters in this book have no existence outside the imagination of the author and have no relation whatsoever to anyone bearing the same name or names. They are not even distantly inspired by any individual known or unknown to the author, and all incidents are pure invention.

This edition published by arrangement with Harlequin Books S.A.

® and TM are trademarks of Harlequin Books S.A., used under license. Trademarks indicated with ® are registered in the United States Patent and Trademark Office, the Canadian Trade Marks Office and in other countries.

Visit Silhouette at www.eHarlequin.com

Printed in U.S.A.

VICTORIA PADE

is a bestselling author of both historical and contemporary romance fiction, and mother of two energetic daughters, Cori and Erin. Although she enjoys her chosen career as a novelist, she occasionally laments that she has never traveled farther from her Colorado home than Disneyland, instead spending all her spare time plugging away at her computer. She takes breaks from writing by indulging in her favorite hobby—eating chocolate.

MANHATTAN MULTIPLES

So much excitement happening at once!

The doors of Manhattan Multiples might shut down. The mayor and Eloise Vale once had a thing. Someone on the staff is pregnant and is keeping it a secret. Romance and drama—and so many babies in the big city!

Michael Dunnigan—Firefighter, devoted son and lover extraordinaire. This confirmed bachelor has no thoughts of matrimony—until he walks into a smoky bar and falls in love at first sight!

Josie Tate—Manhattan Multiples' free-spirited receptionist and impressive poetess can't imagine being tied down, but then she spends a passionate weekend with a sexy fireman and promises to be his pretend fiancée.

Allison Baker—Assistant to Manhattan Multiples' director, this shy beauty hasn't been herself since she went to a party and wound up living out her most romantic fantasy. What could possibly have her on edge these days?

Jorge Perez—The hottest assistant district attorney in Manhattan finally meets the woman he wants, but after their night of passion, she disappears. How fast can a man in love track down his vanishing beauty? Find out in next month's *Practice Makes Pregnant*, Lois Faye Dyer (SE#1569).

Chapter One

"Shh! Don't bark, Pip! You're going to have us living in a cardboard box!" Josie Tate said to her dog as they neared the old, gray stone building where they currently shared an apartment with three friends. An apartment she and Pip were supposed to have vacated.

But did the warning have any effect on the 120-pound, tawny-coated, black-faced bull mastiff who had forced her to take him onto the streets of New York's East Village at midnight? No, it didn't. After one bark and Josie's warning, Pip barked again. And this time they were even closer to the tiny basement apartment directly beneath that of the landlord.

"I mean it, Pip! Be quiet," she begged the animal she'd adopted four months ago when she'd come across the skeletal pet scrounging for food in the trash cans on her way to work.

But again the big dog barked. Three times this round.

"Shh! I mean it!"

There was a no-pets clause in the lease and Josie had already passed the deadline the landlord had given her to get rid of the dog or move out. Waking Mr. Bartholomew now couldn't lead to anything good. Especially not when she hadn't yet found a place she could afford that allowed animals.

Pip seemed to have taken heed because he kept quiet as he crossed what remained of the distance with his nose to the sidewalk, as if he'd picked up the scent of something interesting.

Until he hit the top of the stairs that led down to the apartment.

Then he started to bark with a vengeance. And not the friendly bark. The warning bark he reserved for strangers.

On the other end of the leash, Josie reached the top of the steps behind her dog and finally realized that Pip hadn't merely been barking to hear his own voice. Down below, in the shadows of the unlit stairwell, there was a man standing at her door.

She stopped short just as a light went on in the landlord's apartment and pinch-faced Mr. Bartholomew lunged through the curtains. Then up flew the window so he could shout, "That's it! I want you and that damn dog out of here!"

"I'm sorry, Mr. Bartholomew, but there's a man—"

"I don't care! I need sleep!"

Pip ignored the landlord and continued to bark as Josie thought that if the man in the stairwell was dangerous she wasn't likely to get much help from her irate landlord. But still she said, "But, Mr. Bartholomew, there's some guy—"

"No buts. Either the two of you are gone by tomorrow or I'll get the police to kick the whole lot of you out!"

"It's just me, Josie," her late-night visitor interjected as if he'd been trying to find the opportunity to get a word in edgewise.

She recognized the voice even before she looked from her landlord down the stairs again, and it was enough for her pulse to race and her mind to go blank. But not out of fear.

Pip continued to bark. Mr. Bartholomew went on ranting. But Josie merely stood there at the top of the steps, dumbfounded.

"It's okay, boy, I'm harmless," her midnight visitor said to Pip in a warm, friendly tone as he started up the steps.

Pip must have believed him because the bull mastiff stopped barking, tilted his big square head to one side, and quirked up an ear to stare curiously at him.

The landlord used the sudden silence to shout

louder himself. "Do you hear me? I want you out!"

"Yes, Mr. Bartholomew. I heard you," Josie finally managed to say.

"Tomorrow! Or the other three go, too!"

Josie's visitor was halfway up the stairs and he held out a hand for the dog to sniff. A big hand with long, thick fingers. A big, adept hand. A talented hand that she'd felt all over her body...

Pip allowed their visitor to join them on the landing, sniffing him raptly as the man aimed his gaze up at the landlord and said, "This is my fault. The dog was barking at me. Don't punish them for that."

"They're out," the landlord insisted stubbornly. "She was supposed to be gone a week ago and I'll make sure she goes now. One way or another."

Down went the window with a slam and the landlord disappeared behind the curtains.

"Nice. Real nice," the midnight visitor called after him.

Josie knew she'd have to try persuading the landlord not to enforce his edicts in the morning but since there was nothing she could do about that now, her attention was all on the man who stood only a few inches away, petting her dog.

"Michael Dunnigan," she said as if she couldn't believe her eyes.

"That's me," he responded. "I'm sorry for this—I didn't come here to cause you trouble."

"And yet here you are," Josie said in a questioning tone she hoped might inspire an explanation.

"And yet here I am," he countered instead.

"Not the answer I was looking for."

"The answer to what?" he asked.

She thought he was only playing innocent and opted not to let him get away with it by bluntly demanding, "What are you doing here?"

Michael Dunnigan shrugged mile-wide shoulders negligently and smiled a small smile. "I had sort of a crazy thought tonight and acted on impulse."

"Ah." Josie didn't know what else to say to that and so merely waited for more information.

But rather than getting it, Michael Dunnigan pointed a thumb at the window the landlord had abandoned. "But I don't think we should talk out here."

Josie glanced up at Mr. Bartholomew's window again, as if she expected to find him glaring at them still.

"That *is* your place downstairs, isn't it?" Michael Dunnigan said then. "I knocked but no one answered."

"It's Saturday night. All of my roommates are gone," Josie responded before she realized she'd just negated her best excuse not to ask him in.

He proved the point by saying, "Then can we go inside?"

She was a little worried that this was nothing but a booty call. After all, she'd done something she'd never done in her life when she'd met him—

two weeks ago she'd spent the entire Labor Day weekend with him. In bed.

She still couldn't believe she'd done it. And she'd regretted it ever since. Certainly she had no intention of repeating it. If that's why he was here.

But since she was fresh out of reasons not to let him into the apartment, she had to agree.

"I guess we can go in," she said with a complete lack of enthusiasm. "To talk," she added pointedly.

Apparently he got the message because he held up both hands, palms outward as if in surrender, and said, "Absolutely. Just to talk."

Josie led the way down the stairs, with Pip right beside her and Michael Dunnigan bringing up the rear.

"We have to get that bulb changed," she muttered to herself as she unlocked the door, referring to the light just above the doorway that offered no illumination because the bulb had burned out and not been replaced.

Then she opened the door.

But the moment she stepped inside she was even more sorry she was bringing company with her because she'd forgotten that she'd already unfolded the futon in the living room and made it up for herself for the night.

But what could she do? She couldn't turn around and tell the man she'd just conceded to invite in that she'd changed her mind. She was just going to have to tough this through. And it *would* be tough because having Michael Dunnigan in the same vicinity as a bed was not an easy thing for her even now.

"I was about to call it a night," she said both in explanation and as a hint that she didn't want him to stay long.

Michael Dunnigan closed the door as Josie took off Pip's collar, wishing as she did that she had on something better than her sweat suit over her nightshirt, that she hadn't washed off all her makeup and that she'd at least run a brush through her short bobbed hair before she'd taken Pip on his walk.

But there was nothing to be done about it now. Except to smooth her hair behind her ears once she'd stashed the leash.

"Wow, this place really is small," Michael Dunnigan said as he glanced around.

"There are two bedrooms—two of my roommates share one of them but the other one is really just an oversize closet so only Liz uses it. I lost the toss and ended up sleeping in the living room." She didn't know why she was giving him so many details but the words just seemed to tumble out.

"That's right, I remember you telling me that there are four of you living here. Plus the dog?" Michael Dunnigan asked.

"Four of us and the dog," Josie confirmed. It was one of the very few pieces of information they'd exchanged about themselves during the three-day lovemaking marathon that hadn't left much time—or energy—for conversation.

Josie waited for him to say something else, preferably about why he'd shown up on her doorstep since he still hadn't given her a clue.

But he wasn't forthcoming. Instead he moved to the wall that separated the living room from the hallway-size kitchen.

Josie and her roommates used the wall as a gallery for a mélange of pictures of friends and family and events. As Michael Dunnigan looked at each photograph in turn he was in profile to her and Josie couldn't help taking her own concentrated look at him.

He was still drop-dead gorgeous. More gorgeous than she'd even remembered. He had coal-black hair that he wore short all over. His nose was straight and not too long, and his chin was just pronounced enough. He had high cheekbones and a sharp-cut jawline that was faintly shadowed with the hint of dark stubble.

It was a face that had demanded Josie's attention even through the crowd of the smoky bar where she'd been doing a poetry reading and he'd been sitting in the audience. A face that had riveted her right from the start and kept her enraptured during the three days that had followed. As enraptured as the body that went with it.

The body that was six feet of broad-shouldered, hard-packed muscle that left no doubt that the firefighter was capable of carrying even a full-grown man from a burning building. Six feet of broad-shouldered, hard-packed muscle encased in a pair of tan dress slacks, a hunter green polo shirt, and a sport coat that made Josie suddenly wonder if, when he'd begun this evening, he'd dressed for a date.

"So where are you coming from?" she asked as her curiosity got the better of her.

"A date with my mother's podiatrist," he said without hesitation, a heavy dose of disgust in his tone.

"Another setup?" she asked. One of the few things she knew about him was that his mother was desperate for him to get married and was in relentless pursuit of finding him a wife.

"The fifth setup since I saw you last," he confirmed.

"She's arranged five blind dates for you in two weeks?" Josie said in amazement.

He'd finally finished with the photographs and turned to face her. The full bore of striking green eyes as vibrant as the leaves of summer was almost enough to take her breath away.

But he didn't seem to notice as he answered her question with a complete list. "There was dinner with Mom's hairdresser, lunch with the receptionist from her dentist's office, brunch with the woman who delivered a package to her, coffee with the niece of a friend of her bridge partner, and dinner tonight with the podiatrist."

Josie couldn't help smiling. "You can say one thing—you're eating well."

"Actually, tonight it was tofu cuisine and I hardly ate anything."

And if his tone was any indication, there was more than the food that he hadn't had a taste for.

"So something about tofu cuisine gave you a crazy thought that brought you here," she said, using the segue to maybe finally find out why he'd come when they'd both agreed at the end of that Labor Day weekend that they didn't want any big involvement and to go their separate ways.

Michael Dunnigan smiled at her a bit sheepishly. "It wasn't the tofu, it was the fact that I was sitting across the table from this woman whose company I was not enjoying in the least, thinking that if I had to do one more blind date I would scream, and wondering how the hell I was going to get my mother to stop."

"And that gave you a crazy idea."

"A really crazy idea."

But still he didn't tell her what that crazy idea was.

He took another look around the apartment, shook his head and said, "I can't believe four people and a dog are crammed in here."

Josie clenched her teeth and shrieked to let her frustration be known. "What was the crazy idea?" she said, slowly enunciating each word.

Michael Dunnigan smiled again, obviously enjoying this. "It occurred to me that my mother is never going to cease and desist until she actually believes I've found someone."

And that made him think of me?

A hopeful little flutter in the pit of her stomach gave Josie pause.

Yes, she had liked Michael Dunnigan. A lot. Yes, she'd been attracted to him. A lot. But she hadn't been kidding Labor Day weekend—she was strictly against getting involved with anyone, so she'd nixed any idea of a relationship developing between them. Which, for his own reasons, he'd been in favor of. So why was she feeling flattered and hopeful that he'd connected *finding someone* with her?

She tamped down the very notion.

"Okay," she said to prompt him. "Your mother is never going to cease and desist until she believes you've found someone. That seems logical."

"It does, doesn't it? I don't know why it took me so long to realize it. Anyway," he went on, "that was when I started to think about the bind you said you were in to find another place to live and I thought that if you hadn't already done that, what if we solved each other's problems?"

"You've lost me," she confessed.

"Well…" He shook his head as if he couldn't believe what he was about to say. "Remember, I warned you that it was crazy."

"Uh-huh."

"Well, I thought, what if I sort of hire you to move in with me and pretend to be my fiancée?"

That just made Josie laugh.

"Okay, so it's a crazy and funny idea," he said. But he wasn't laughing along with her. He was just waiting for her to stop.

So she did. And that was when she said, "You want me to move in with you?" as if it just had to be a joke.

"On a purely platonic basis," he was quick to

add. "Of course my mother wouldn't know it, but you'd have your own room—rent free—plus use of the rest of the place. Which includes a small yard the dog could go out into. You'd have to play the part of my fiancée when my mother came around or if I needed your attendance at something, but the reality would be that we'd just be roommates. And the beauty of it is that if my mother believes I'm engaged to you, I could get her off my back."

"That really is a crazy idea," Josie said.

He smiled sheepishly again and she wished he would stop it. Smiling put lines at the corners of each of his eyes and deep grooves bracketing his supple mouth, and only made him more attractive.

"We could tell my mother that since we really just met we're going to have an extended engagement," he continued as if this were actually a possibility. "And who knows how long we could draw it out? No matter how long it is, it'll give me a break."

He sounded like he needed one.

Certainly she needed a place to move to...

Josie could hardly believe that last thought had gone through her head.

Was she honestly considering this?

"It's crazy," she repeated. Only now what seemed even crazier than his idea was the fact that she might be thinking about doing it.

"I thought being a little crazy was right up your alley," he commented then, as if he liked that about her.

She'd never considered herself crazy. Spontaneous. Free-spirited. Adventurous. Those were all things she remembered of her parents. Things she liked to keep alive in herself. And even if some people—like Mr. Bartholomew—considered what she did on the spur of the moment or on a whim crazy, what was important to her was that *she* found her actions reasonable. Or enjoyable. Or beneficial to someone.

Moving in with Michael Dunnigan, pretending to be engaged to him, would be beneficial to him, a little voice in the back of her mind pointed out. It would also be beneficial to her....

"Have you been drinking?" she asked suddenly, wanting to make sure this wasn't some inebriated lark that he would regret when he sobered up.

"Drinking with Miss Tofu? Are you kidding? She ordered me a shot of some thick green stuff—wheat grass juice of something—but there was definitely no liquor in it. It might have tasted better if there had been."

She purposely hadn't invited him to sit down. Or sat herself for that matter. But now he perched a casual hip on the arm of an easy chair as if he were right at home anyway.

Then he said, "It wouldn't be all that complicated. An occasional meal with my family. Holidays. A wedding or a reunion or a birthday here and there. And you wouldn't always have to go to everything with me. Sometimes I could just say you had to work or you didn't feel well or something else came up. The rest of the time we'd go our separate ways. Date. Do our own thing the same as any roommates. Plus my shifts run twenty-four on, twenty-four off, so every other day—and night—you'd have the place to yourself. And think how happy you'd make Mom,'' he finished with another of those smiles that weakened Josie's knees.

And that was the biggest problem with this idea, she thought when it happened. Sparks had already flown between them. She already knew there was an attraction between them. A combustible attraction. An uncontrollable attraction. The kind of attraction that had landed her in bed with him for the most passionate, the most mind-boggling sex she'd ever experienced. How could she now move in with him, be in close proximity to him, play at being in a romantic relationship with him, and keep it platonic?

''I don't think it would be very wise,'' she said in response to her own misgivings.

Which he seemed to read like an open book. ''Because of Labor Day weekend. I know, I've thought about that. It was pretty fantastic and it would be hard…difficult to avoid the temptation to repeat it. But we've already agreed that that isn't what we want and so far we've stuck to it. We haven't seen each other again. And believe me, I've thought about calling you. So I think that if we make a pact just to be roommates, friends—''

''Coconspirators.''

''Okay, coconspirators and partners in crime, and we really put our minds to it, we can keep

Labor Day weekend in the past and stay this new course for the future.''

Josie didn't have time for a rebuttal because there was a loud pounding on her door just then.

She crossed back to it and opened it, too lost in her own thoughts to ask who it was first. But even so she was surprised to find Mr. Bartholomew standing outside in the stairwell. Still looking furious.

"Here," he said, shoving a sheet of paper at her. "I called my lawyer—"

"At midnight on a Saturday night?"

"If I can't sleep, neither can anyone else!" the paunchy man in the undershirt snarled. "My lawyer says to put in writing that you've broken the lease and either you get out or I can evict you, your dog, and the rest of the occupants of this apartment. So there it is. You're gone tomorrow or else. Legally."

Josie had no idea if he was bluffing or not but the landlord turned tail and stormed up the stairs, leaving her with a handwritten paper saying just what he'd told her it said.

So much for trying to cajole him into letting her stay a little longer.

She closed the door but remained facing it for a while, staring at it and considering her options.

She could get rid of Pip.

But she loved the big bull mastiff and she wasn't going to do that.

She could gamble that Mr. Bartholomew couldn't really evict her the next day and that maybe she could find a place for them before he actually could throw them out.

But if she was wrong he could very well kick out her three roommates, too, and that wasn't fair. Besides the fact that she honestly could end up on the street because if the landlord did evict her suddenly she doubted a hotel or the YWCA could let her in with a dog.

Or she could take Michael Dunnigan up on his offer.

She could move into his brownstone, live rent free, and pretend to be his fiancée.

Actually, it didn't seem as if she did have any options.

"Do you absolutely, positively guarantee that this will be a purely platonic arrangement?" she heard herself say before she'd even turned around to face Michael Dunnigan again.

"I absolutely, positively guarantee it. You'll never even see me without a shirt on."

Josie closed her eyes as if that might keep her from seeing the image that came into her head at just the mention of him bare-chested. The image of him in the kitchen between lovemaking sessions over Labor Day, eating out of a carton, nothing on but a pair of boxer shorts, his V-shaped torso a work of art...

"I don't even want to see you without shoes and socks," she said almost as if she were in pain.

"Okay. Not even without shoes and socks," he agreed.

Josie opened her eyes and took a deep breath,

sighing it out resolutely. "All right," she said softly. "I guess we can give it a try since I don't have anywhere else to go. But just for the record, I'm not happy about lying to your mother."

"I'm not happy about it, either. But she won't listen to me when I explain why I can't get married and have kids right now."

Funny, but after their Labor Day weekend together, Josie had had the impression that he simply hadn't wanted to be tied down. But something in what he'd just said made her think there was more to it than that.

Of course she'd said basically the same thing to him and she had reasons that ran deeper, too.

But it was too late to get into all of that now so she let it lay and finally turned away from the door.

"I guess we have a deal then," she said, looking at that oh-so-handsome face and hoping they really could abide by their pact.

He smiled again, a thousand-watt grin that made her doubt her own willpower already. "So, will you marry me?" he said, joking.

Josie rolled her eyes. "Well, I'll make it look like I will, anyway."

"Good enough."

"I guess I'll have to move in tomorrow," she said with a nod back at the door where Mr. Bartholomew had just appeared and disappeared. "How are you going to explain to your mother that you went out with her podiatrist on Saturday night and have a live-in fiancée on Sunday?"

"I'll make up something. She'll be so thrilled she won't pay attention to too many details."

"So when do you want me?" Poor choice of words. "I mean, what time do you want me to move in?"

"Anytime. Do you need a truck or something for furniture?"

"I only own what I can fit into my car."

"That works. I'm fully furnished."

Somehow that sounded like a double entendre but since he'd let her slip of the tongue slide, she didn't comment on his.

"So, I guess that's it," he added. "I'll see you when you get there tomorrow."

"I'll have to pack my stuff and load the car so it probably won't be until the evening."

"Whatever. I'll be there," he assured.

He got up from the arm of the chair and headed for the door himself.

But before he reached it, he paused near enough to Josie for her to smell the scent of his aftershave. Near enough to bend and, with a warm brush of his breath against her ear, say, "Want to seal our engagement with a kiss?"

Josie gave him a withering look that made him laugh this time.

"Just kidding," he assured as he straightened and went the rest of the way to the door.

But with one hand on the knob he smiled at her yet again and said, "Thanks for this. You don't know what a relief it is to think that I'll be free of my mother's matchmaking."

"It's a relief to me to have somewhere to go with Pip," she admitted.

Although that wasn't completely true.

Because while it *was* a relief to know she finally had a place to live peacefully with her dog, she was still worried about who she'd be living with in that place.

And as Michael Dunnigan finally left she had to wonder if she hadn't just exchanged one set of problems for another.

Chapter Two

"How was the date? Didn't you just love her?"

"Hello to you, too, Ma," Michael said in order to avoid answering his mother's questions when he arrived at her home at ten o'clock Sunday morning. She lived only blocks away from his brownstone in Brooklyn.

His mother was standing at the stove in her kitchen. As she did every Sunday morning, the five-foot-two compact powerhouse of a woman was making pancakes. She had on a purple velour sweat suit, elaborate makeup, and her head was still swathed from the night before in the toilet paper turban that preserved the bouffant, flipped-at-the-ends hairdo sported by every woman who went to the neighborhood salon.

''Will you take that stuff off your head?'' Michael added after he'd leaned over to kiss his mother's cheek.

Elsa Dunnigan slid golden brown pancakes from the griddle, ladled more batter onto the hot surface, and then obliged her son by unwrapping her black hair. With the exception of being slightly flat in the back it remained an undisturbed helmet.

''The date, Mikey. I want to hear about the date.''

Michael picked up the already poured glass of orange juice at his spot at the red-and-silver kitchen table and took a drink, noting as he did that there were only two place settings. Unless Michael was working, Sunday breakfast was the one meal each week that he, his mother and his younger sister always tried to have together. So again he ignored his mother's query in favor of one of his own.

''Cindy isn't eating with us?''

''She had to go to a bridal shower brunch in the city,'' Elsa said as if the entire subject of her other child was inconsequential. But as she took a platter filled with bacon and sausages from where it was being kept warm in the oven and brought that, a dish of pancakes and another plate of fried eggs to the table, she said, ''And if you don't answer me right now I'm going to call Dr. Miranda myself and tell her you had such a fabulous time with her last night that you want to see her again tonight.''

Michael knew his mother would do just that so he stopped hedging as they both sat at the table.

"The date was good and bad—the bad being the date itself and the good being that it made me realize something and take a big step."

He'd planned this out on the way home from Josie Tate's apartment the previous night so he knew exactly how he was going to explain the sudden turn of events.

"I don't understand," his mother said. "You didn't like Dr. Miranda?"

"No, Ma."

Elsa Dunnigan frowned at him so fiercely it made her eyes squint and nearly disappear in the lines around them.

"She's a nice girl," his mother insisted. "A professional woman with a thriving medical practice. She wants to get married. She wants babies. She'll make a good wife. She can't help it if she has sinus problems and has to blow her nose every five minutes. And those ears could be covered if she'd just let her hair grow over them. I could set her up with Cissy—now that I've finally smoothed the waters after you never called *her* back, either. Cissy could do Dr. Miranda's hair so no one would ever see those Dumbo ears."

Cissy was Elsa's beautician. She wore her hair even bigger and more rock-solid than any of her clients. Michael had spent the whole blind date with her wondering how she could not notice that the style was outdated by at least twenty years. And when he coupled the hair with the nearly Geisha-like makeup, the gum popping, the honking laugh, the dagger fingernails she'd used in lieu of a fork to pick up strands of spaghetti, and the fact that they'd had absolutely nothing in common, it had not been a date he'd wanted to repeat. So he hadn't called her again. Much to his mother's dismay.

But actually, just the thought of that date and the date the night before pushed him to finally tell his mother the story he'd come up with to free himself from any future setups.

"I'm engaged," he announced.

Elsa made a very unflattering sound in response. Something like "Puh!"

Clearly she didn't believe him.

"To Dr. Miranda?" she asked facetiously.

"No, not to Miranda. I told you I didn't like her so you're out of luck when it comes to free callus scrapings," Michael informed her.

"Then who are you engaged to? As if I'm buying this load of horse manure."

"Get out your checkbook because it's true. I am engaged," he said, enunciating each word slowly, as if to better get it to sink in.

"To who?" his mother said the same way.

"You don't know her," Michael answered calmly. He knew this was risky business. He'd never been an adept liar. And his mother had always been able to see through it when he'd tried. But now he had enough at stake to make him determined to pull it off. "Her name is Josie Tate. She's the receptionist at that Manhattan Multiples place—remember, it was written up in the newspapers a few months ago? They help women who are pregnant with more than one baby or something. You showed me the article yourself—''

''I remember. My friend Agnes's daughter went there when she was going to have triplets,'' Elsa said, conceding that she knew what he was talking about but still sounding suspicious of his claim to be engaged.

''Well, Josie works there. We met the Friday night before Labor Day.''

''That was the night I arranged a date with my insurance agent's secretary,'' Elsa said to let him know he wasn't putting anything over on her.

''Yes and Sharon McKinty is one of Josie's roommates. She took me to a bar that night where Josie was reading poetry—poetry she wrote herself.''

It wasn't easy to come up with a whole lot of information about his new fiancée because Michael didn't know much about her. He was just trying to sound knowledgeable with what little he had learned over Labor Day weekend.

''You went out with Sharon McKinty and ended up with someone else?'' his mother asked.

As a matter of fact.

''Sharon McKinty met up with an old boyfriend and deserted me. I told you that. But I stuck around to hear more of Josie's poetry and when she was finished we…well, we hit it off.''

That was all true. Although to say that he and Josie Tate had hit it off was something of an understatement.

''You told me Sharon dumped you,'' his mother

confirmed. "But you didn't tell me you'd met someone else." More suspicion.

"I wanted to keep this one to myself," he said, as if Josie had just been too good to share when in fact meeting somebody in a bar and spending three days in bed with them was hardly a story to tell your mother. Even if it had been the best three days he'd ever spent. With anyone.

But despite Michael's best attempt to make keeping Josie a secret sound romantic, his mother said, "Why did you want to keep it to yourself? Is there something wrong with her? Won't I like her?"

"I wanted to keep her to myself because she's just very special."

That was no lie. Josie Tate *did* seem special. Special enough that after their weekend together he'd thought that to see her again could be too great a test of the vow he'd made to himself.

Michael had only told his mother once why he was resistant to her greatest desire—that he find a wife and have a family. Elsa had discounted it as silly and promptly disregarded it, but his reasons were strong nevertheless.

As a volunteer firefighter, his father had been killed in a burning building when Michael was only twelve. Being left without a dad had been tougher on him than he'd ever let his mother know. And then, when the World Trade Center bombings had happened and so many of his brother firefighters had been lost, when he'd seen so many wives, so many children, left behind, Michael had decided that if he was going to do this job he loved, he was not going to chance leaving behind a wife or a child.

Whether his mother liked it or not.

And the pure power of his attraction to Josie that weekend had seemed like something to avoid if he was serious about it. Which he was.

"So how is this girl special enough that you met her two weeks ago and left my podiatrist last night to get engaged to her without even telling me you knew her?" Elsa demanded.

"How is Josie special?" he repeated, thinking about it as he finished his third pancake. "Well, she's great-looking, for one thing."

"What does she look like?"

"She has the shiniest hair I've ever seen. Light brown with blond streaks that make it seem kind of sunny. She wears it short—about to her chin—and it's smooth and soft and sleek. And she has this way of brushing it behind her ears that's...I don't know...just so damn cute."

"What color eyes does she have?" his mother demanded, as if this were a test.

But if it was, it was a test he could pass because he knew very well what Josie looked like: He'd pictured her in his mind's eye a million times in the past two weeks.

"She has blue eyes. So blue—so *bright* blue— that they're almost electric. Plus her skin is like cream. And she has a tiny nose—but not *too* tiny, just right, really. And she has good teeth—white and straight—and lips that are this natural pink that doesn't even need lipstick. She has a great smile. And she's thin but not too thin and—''

''So it's all about looks?'' his mother cut in, pulling him from the image of Josie Tate that he'd been slightly carried away by.

''No, it's not all about looks,'' he said. ''I'm just describing her to you because that's what you asked me. She's also sweet and smart—she writes poetry that just blows you away. She's funny. She has a great sense of humor. She doesn't make big deals out of small stuff. She's free and open and easygoing. She has a terrific outlook on life—'' And maybe, even though he didn't know a single thing about where she came from or what her goals were or anything about her family or her romantic history or where she saw herself in five years, he did know slightly more about her than he'd thought.

''It sounds like she just bowled you over,'' Elsa finished for him, beginning to sound more open to this whole thing.

''She did bowl me over,'' Michael agreed, realizing there was some truth to that, too. Even if he didn't really want to admit it.

''Anyway,'' he added, getting back to his pre-planned speech, ''We've spent some time together since Labor Day but I wanted to keep it—to keep *her*—to myself. So I didn't tell you about it. I went on the rest of those dates you set up to see if I still might find someone I liked better. But last night I was sitting across from your podiatrist wondering why I was wasting my time. Thinking that Josie is who I want to be with. The *only* person I want to be with. And that I needed to do something about it no matter how short a time we've known each other.''

That was a mixture of lies and truth. He hadn't seen anything of Josie Tate since Labor Day weekend—that was a lie. But he had compared every other woman since then to her. And even with the little he knew about her, every other woman had still come up short, so that part was true. No, it hadn't convinced him to propose for real. But sitting across from the podiatrist, not enjoying himself in the slightest, *had* made him think about Josie Tate. It had inspired the idea to solve both her housing problem and his mother problem by suggesting the fake engagement.

"So you left my podiatrist and went and asked this other girl to marry you?" his mother said.

"I didn't just *leave* your podiatrist. I took her home. But then I went to Josie's place and... Well, we're engaged and she's moving in today."

Elsa's eyebrows arched at that. "Two weeks is all you've known this girl and you're engaged *and* she's moving in with you?"

"That's right."

His mother pushed her nearly empty plate away and seemed to mull that over before she said, "You're serious? You're getting married?"

"Not anytime soon," Michael was quick to say. Maybe too quick. "I mean, we've fallen head over heels but we *did* just meet. We want to take some time to really get to know each other before we actually get married. A long engagement—that's what she wants, that's what I want.''

''I don't think you should count on that. If this girl works every day with mothers-to-be and new babies, she's bound to start wanting a baby of her own.''

There was a note of optimism in his mother's tone that let him know she was not only coming to believe him but that she was beginning to warm to the idea of his whirlwind romance.

''We'll cross that bridge when we come to it. *If* we come to it,'' Michael said. ''For now, we both just want to settle in together and honestly get to know each other.''

''And she's a good girl? Not some fly-by-night who's taking advantage of you or will disappear with your credit card and your furniture while you're at work?''

''Sharon McKinty introduced us and *you* arranged the date with her,'' Michael pointed out.

''Did Sharon vouch for her?''

''Sharon vouched for us both—she told Josie that I'm a stand-up guy from a good family with a mother who has big hair—''

''I don't have *big* hair. I have a *lot* of hair.'' Elsa defended herself from his teasing.

''Uh-huh,'' Michael said sarcastically before he continued. ''And Sharon told me that Josie is the best roommate she's ever had, that she's the kind of person who takes in stray animals, donates blood, volunteers at the soup kitchen, brings coffee to the homeless guy on the corner every morning, and would give her last dime away if she thought somebody needed it more than she did. I don't think I have to worry about her running off with my furniture or my credit card.''

''And you love her and she loves you?''

That one made him very uncomfortable. ''We got engaged last night, didn't we?'' he said as if that was answer enough.

Apparently it was because his mother said, ''It must have been love at first sight.''

Certainly it had been attraction at first sight. He hadn't been able to keep his eyes off Josie that night at the bar. In fact, he'd been almost mesmerized by her. But that wasn't important now. Now they were only going to be roommates and friends—that was something he needed not to forget.

''When do I get to meet her?'' his mother asked then, finally sounding convinced and happy about the fact that Michael had found someone.

''Maybe in a day or two. Let's let her get moved in and—''

''Tomorrow,'' Elsa decreed. ''We'll have dinner. I'll cook.''

''I'd need to check with Josie. I don't want you giving her the bum's rush, Ma. She'll be around a long time.''

''I have to meet the girl who's going to be my daughter-in-law, don't I?''

''You will. Believe me, you will.''

''Tomorrow. See if we can meet tomorrow,'' Elsa insisted forcefully.

Michael took a deep breath and sighed it out with resignation. His mother was nothing if not persistent. And pushy. Which was why, he reminded himself, he'd felt the need to concoct this plan in the first place.

But that still didn't keep him from feeling guilty for perpetrating this sham on her.

He just didn't know what else to do to get her to back off.

"Tomorrow," he conceded. "I'll see if you can meet Josie tomorrow."

Elsa sat back in her chair, looking pleased. "Good. Tomorrow night for dinner," she said with as much finality as if Michael had agreed to it.

"I don't know about a whole meal. Why don't I just bring her by for a few minutes the first time?"

It was as if Elsa hadn't heard him. "Dinner here at seven," she dictated. "I'll even get wine."

His mother got up and went to the drawer beside the sink where she took out a tablet and a pen and began to make a list that Michael had no doubt was for groceries she would go to the store and buy before the day was over in spite of everything he'd said about checking with Josie first.

But he knew better than to waste any more effort on trying to slow the runaway train that was his mother. And as he stood and started to clear the table all he could think was, *You don't have any idea what you've gotten yourself into, Josie Tate....*

He just hoped she really was as easygoing as he'd said she was, as easygoing as she'd seemed.

Because it was the only way she was likely to get through this.

It was seven o'clock Sunday evening before Josie was completely loaded up and ready to go. The trunk and rear seat of her small vintage sedan were crammed full of her clothes and belongings, and Pip was sitting regally in the passenger seat, staring straight ahead, patiently awaiting his ride while she said goodbye to Sharon.

"You're sure about this?" asked the only one of her three roommates she was close to.

"Hey, I spent a whole weekend with this guy on your say-so that he wasn't a psycho," Josie joked. "Are you telling me now that he is?"

"No. For the two years I've worked for his mother's insurance carrier, I've been listening to the woman brag about him and he's anything but a psycho. He's a decorated firefighter and I think the Boy Scouts gave him some kind of award, too. If I hadn't met up with T.J. that night and he hadn't apologized, I might have given Michael Dunnigan a go-round myself. But just because he's not a psycho doesn't mean you should be moving into his place and pretending to be engaged to him."

"Remember, don't blow this if you talk to his mother," Josie warned, wondering if she should have been quite so honest with her friend.

"Believe me, his mother does all the talking," Sharon assured her. "But still, actually moving in with him? And acting as if the two of you are getting married? That's pretty weird.''

''It'll be okay. Besides, old sourpuss Bartholomew didn't give me any other choice. He's even up there at his window now, making sure I'm leaving,'' she added with a poke of her chin at the building behind her friend.

''Maybe we could have hidden Pip,'' Sharon suggested.

Josie laughed at that. ''Where? How?''

Sharon shrugged. ''Oh, I don't know. This whole thing just doesn't seem fair.''

''It's more fair than getting you guys all evicted because of Pip and me. Don't worry about it. Now that I have somewhere to go, it isn't a big deal.''

''Yes, it is a big deal when it means you're going to have to play at being engaged to accomplish it. When you're going to pull the wool over the eyes of Michael Dunnigan's mother, of all people. Everything with that woman is a big deal. She's a steamroller in panty hose. You might start out only pretending to be engaged, but before Elsa Dunnigan is through, you're liable to find yourself married with ten kids. And if she finds out this is just a scam? I don't even want to think what she might do.'' Sharon ended with wide eyes to emphasize the terror of just considering that possibility.

But Josie just laughed again. ''Come on. She can't be that bad.''

''She can and she is. I wouldn't want her for even a *pretend* mother-in-law. That night that I went out with Michael I kept looking at him, thinking that he might be gorgeous but I wouldn't go near him for anything but a one-nighter because nothing is worth putting up with that woman more than I have to at the office.''

"If she's that horrible why did you agree to go out with her son in the first place?" Josie challenged.

"I was mad at T.J. and I wanted to teach him a lesson. But I'm telling you, Josie, I thought my mother was a pain in the neck, but Elsa Dunnigan has her beat by a mile.''

"I won't be living with his mother," Josie pointed out.

"No, you'll be trying to live platonically with a guy who's already swept you off your feet and into his bed. On top of the whole mother thing. It's like double jeopardy.''

"What happened between Michael and me over Labor Day is history. I only slept with him because... Well, it was just a bad weekend for me. The anniversary of my parents' death is always dicey. But what happened before won't happen again.''

"I know you needed comfort and solace and forgetfulness that weekend, but still, Michael Dunnigan is some pretty powerful stuff. I don't know if you can just blame that three-day marathon on being bummed out. Or trust that *not* being bummed out will make you immune.''

"Determination not to repeat that marathon is what will make me immune. And it will help that we'll be going our separate ways. He'll be completely out of the house every other day. Believe me, nothing is going to happen between us again.''

Sharon didn't look convinced. Or sound it when she said, ''Whatever you say.''

''I say it'll be just fine,'' Josie said with conviction.

And by then she honestly believed it would be. She'd thought long and hard about this situation since the man in question had left the previous night. And, in spite of his appeal, there were two very large roadblocks to her ever wanting to get seriously involved with him. And neither of them had anything to do with his mother.

In the first place, Josie had no intention of changing her own unencumbered lifestyle.

And in the second place, Michael's job was the cure for even contemplating any kind of involvement with him whatsoever.

No matter how attractive he was, how sexy, how funny or fun or intelligent or charming or well put-together, Josie had one steadfast rule—she was absolutely not going to let herself get involved with a guy in a high-risk profession. She knew firsthand the devastation that could be wreaked if the worst occurred in life, and although she realized that anyone could have any kind of freakish accident at any time, being connected to someone who courted danger through their work was more risky than she could bear. Which meant that Michael Dunnigan was one very off-limits man.

''I should get going,'' she told Sharon. ''I still have to unpack all this stuff when I get there.''

Sharon nodded her resignation. "You'll call me this week?" her friend said.

"I will. Maybe we can meet for lunch one day."

"Good. And you know, if this doesn't work out, you can always find Pip a nice home and come back."

"It'll be fine," Josie repeated.

"Or, if the temptation gets to be too much, you could stay there on the nights Michael works but leave Pip there and spend the night here with us on Michael's days off."

"There's an idea," Josie said, thinking that might actually be something she would do if the attraction to Michael started to get the best of her. Certainly she would do that before she would repeat Labor Day weekend.

She and Sharon hugged then.

"I'm going to miss you, though," Sharon said, sounding on the verge of tears. "I hate that you won't be here to make me your famous chai tea when I come home stressed."

"I can probably talk you through making it yourself in an emergency," Josie joked again, this time somewhat feebly.

Their hug ended and Sharon leaned over to the window beside Pip. "'Bye, puppy," she said to the large animal. "Be a good boy and don't get your mom into any more trouble."

Pip had turned his head toward her when she'd first spoken to him and he gave the window one lick as if it were Sharon's face. Then he went back to staring straight ahead.

"Damn Bartholomew," Sharon muttered as she straightened. Then, to Josie, she said, "Drive safely."

"I will."

Josie headed around the front of the car to the driver's side. "I'll talk to you this week," she called as she got in behind the wheel.

Sharon moved back from the curb, waving as Josie pulled out into the street.

"Here we go, big dog, another of life's adventures," she announced to Pip as she drove away.

At least that's what she hoped the feeling she was having was—excitement for a new experience, a new adventure. Better that than feeling excited over getting to see Michael Dunnigan again.

Josie looked at all of life as an adventure. She liked to keep things free and easy. She liked to try new and different foods. She liked to meet new people. She liked to pick up on the spur of the moment and go somewhere without having anything planned, without knowing where she was going or what she was going to do or when she would come back. She liked to change jobs. To have new experiences. All of that excited her. Thrilled her. The same way it had excited and thrilled her parents.

But anything dangerous, anything life-threatening—that was something else again. And that was where she was different from her parents.

But then she'd lived through the consequences of their thrill-seeking. And they hadn't.

When Sharon had introduced her to Michael

Dunnigan that Friday night before Labor Day, Sharon hadn't told her he was a firefighter. If she had, Josie would likely not have said more than a brief hello to him—that's how adamant she was about steering clear of anyone who was into anything high-risk.

But as it was, Josie hadn't learned what Michael did for a living until late in their weekend together. And the moment she'd discovered it, their encounter had turned temporary in her mind. Because if there was one thing she knew for certain, it was that she didn't want any permanent connection to anyone who did things that could be life-threatening.

Attachment issues—that's what a psychologist she'd once dated had said about her—that she had attachment issues.

But Josie liked to think of it as independence. She was proud of how self-sufficient she was. She certainly didn't see anything wrong with maintaining that independence and self-sufficiency.

And if she was particularly adamant about steering clear of anyone who put themselves, their entire life, on the line every day? She considered that a lesson life had taught her at a young age.

"So you and I are only going to be friends, Michael Dunnigan," she said out loud, as if that would make it an irrefutable fact.

Pip went from angling his blunt black nose up at the small gap she'd left in the window so he could enjoy the smells along the way, to looking at her as if he wasn't buying that for a minute.

"I mean it," she said decisively to convince him. "Friends. Roommates. That's it."

And if she already knew that wasn't going to be an easy thing to pull off because the man had hardly been out of her thoughts at all in the two weeks since they'd parted ways?

Well, she liked a challenge, too.

Maybe not quite as much as she liked Michael Dunnigan, but still...

"I should probably be grateful if he has a dragon lady for a mother," she said to Pip. "Maybe it'll help cool me off to him."

But dragon lady or no dragon lady, Josie really was bent on being nothing but friends and roommates with Michael Dunnigan. No matter what it took.

Because even if she wasn't determined to remain unattached to any one person, even if she wasn't fiercely protective of her independence, any man whose job put her in a position where, on the turn of a dime, she might be abandoned again the way her parents' deaths had abandoned her, was not the man for her. No matter what.

And since the closer she got to Michael's house, the closer she got to Michael, the more butterflies took wing in her stomach and the more eager she felt, she thought that maybe it would be a good thing if his mother really was a dragon lady.

Because she just might need all the help she could get to turn herself off to Michael Dunnigan.

It was dusk by the time Josie arrived at Michael's brownstone. Luckily she found a parking spot right across the street so she didn't have to double park to unload her car.

But once she'd maneuvered the sedan between the truck and the station wagon at the curb and turned off the engine, she didn't rush out of the vehicle. Instead she sat there and studied the place she remembered from the last time she'd been here.

Ten steps edged by a black wrought-iron railing led up to the double-door entrance of the stately two-story brown brick building. The entrance was sheltered by an arched overhang decorated with pilasters that ran along either side and ended at two ornate brackets that connected each pilaster to the frieze.

There were twin carriage lamps on the pilasters and another inside the uppermost curve of the arch. All of them were lit to welcome her and more light shone through the ovals of beveled glass in the center of each dark walnut door.

To the right of the entrance was a large bay window that Josie remembered well. Both the front door and the window were in the living room. She and Michael hadn't been able to contain themselves long enough to get to his bedroom the first time they'd made love so they'd ended up barely getting through the door and onto the floor just below that bay window.

The memory flooded through Josie's mind unexpectedly and caught her off guard. The memory of tearing each other's clothes off while mouths clung together. Of urgent, exploring hands. Of bodies colliding in hungry need...

Not a good thing to think about, she knew, and she worked to block the memory, the images, the recollection of sensations and feelings and things that made her crave reliving it all.

Then Pip offered a distraction by whining to let her know he wanted out of the car now that it was no longer moving.

Josie took a deep breath, sighed and said, "Okay. I guess you're right. We're home. For better or worse."

She attached Pip's leash to the metal loop on his harness but left him sitting there as she got out of her side of the car. Then she went around to the passenger door to let Pip out that way.

With his blunt nose to the ground, Josie led the bull mastiff across the street that ran in front of the row of nearly identical homes. As if he'd been there before, Pip promptly climbed the ten steps to Michael's brownstone.

Michael must have been watching for them because before Josie could ring the bell, the door opened and there he was.

"Oh. Hi," she said a bit dimly.

Even though he hadn't dressed up for her arrival he was freshly shaved. The heady smell of clean mountain-air-scented aftershave drifted to her nostrils as she took in the sight of him in a plain white T-shirt that was tight enough to hug his chest, shoulders and biceps and the sweatpants that let

her know there were muscular thighs hidden inside them.

In fact, not only couldn't she keep from taking
in the sight, one look at him made her heart skip
a beat and she thought that it might have been
better if he *had* dressed up. Maybe slacks and a
shirt would have hidden more and given her a
break. But as it was, his clothes seemed like a scant
barrier between her and that body she remembered
all too well.

"Welcome to your new home," he said in response to her greeting, stepping aside to allow her
and the dog inside.

But Josie hesitated.

Somehow she hadn't thought that being there
again, with him, would bring so much to the surface. But suddenly she was having difficulty *not*
thinking about Labor Day weekend. About repeating it…

Roommates, she reminded herself. Nothing but
roommates…

Roommates who usually provided their own an-
noyances. Like stinky tennis shoes. Cupboard
doors left open. Drinking out of the milk carton.
Dirty dishes in the sink. The toilet seat left up.

Those were all things that made roommates un-
appealing. So maybe if every time she started to
notice what she shouldn't be noticing about Michael, she thought about the grossest, most dis-
gusting thing a roommate had ever done, it would
turn her off to even him…

Toenail clippings on the coffee table—that had

been the worst. So that was what she would think about.

Toenail clippings. Toenail clippings. Toenail clippings...

It helped. At least enough to get her through the front door.

"Are you okay?" Michael asked as she belatedly stepped inside.

He was smiling a confused sort of smile and there were two creases between his full eyebrows that let her know he'd seen her hesitancy.

"It's just a little strange," she told him.

"I know. For me, too. But I think that will go away."

It'll go away if I imagine you leaving toenail clippings on the coffee table....

"Anyhow," he said then, "I thought we could put the dog out back so we can keep the door open while we bring in your stuff."

"We?"

"I'm not going to let you do it alone," Michael informed her.

That was nice. And above and beyond the call of duty for a mere roommate. But Josie was a little concerned with the precedent it might set if he acted like a boyfriend. So she said, "You really don't have to. It's only clothes and some boxes. There isn't furniture or anything. I like to keep encumbrances to a minimum."

"Well, I can't just sit and watch."

No, that definitely wouldn't be an improvement. Not when she could almost feel those penetrating green eyes on her every time he looked her way. Not when they turned the heat up on her whole body.

Besides, she reasoned, the sooner she unloaded her car and could lock herself in her own room—away from Michael and his effect on her—the better. So she conceded. "Okay. Thanks, I'd appreciate the help."

"Good. Then let's get the dog out back."

Michael led the way across the living room that was decorated sparsely in brown leather and oak, to the swinging door that connected the kitchen and dining room. The back door was between the two and after Josie had removed Pip's leash, the big dog was only too happy to go out to investigate his new domain.

Then Josie and Michael retraced their steps and began the process of getting her moved in.

Her room was to be the one across the hall from his and she advised him to just leave the boxes on the floor there and the clothes on the double bed with the white chenille spread.

He did as he was told and with the exception of a comment here and there, they worked without saying much.

By shortly before nine they were finished, but rather than Michael saying a simple good-night and leaving her to her own devices, he said, "How about a glass of wine to toast our new living arrangement while we sort through the details?"

"The details?"

"I always think sharing space goes better if you talk about some things up front."

Josie was a free-and-easy kind of person, which was how she approached everything, so she'd always just addressed the details of living with other people when they cropped up. But if he liked to set ground rules at the start, she was okay with that, too. The wine, on the other hand? She wasn't too sure about the wisdom in that.

"I have to work tomorrow so maybe I should pass on the wine," she said.

"Come on, one glass isn't going to do any harm," he insisted, not waiting for her to decline a second time before he headed out of her room.

There were two sets of stairs leading from the second level—stairs with a beautifully carved oak banister that descended into the living room, and much plainer, more serviceable steps that led to the kitchen. It was the kitchen stairs that Josie followed Michael down, trying not to notice his to-die-for derriere as she did.

While he poured two glasses of the Riesling, Josie let Pip in and filled the water bowl she'd brought with her from one of her boxes in the bedroom.

"Where shall I put this?" she asked Michael, holding up the dog dish.

"How about alongside the counter near the door? That should be out of the way enough to keep us from spilling it."

Josie placed the bowl where Michael had suggested and then turned back to him to accept the wine.

"Here's to us," he said, touching his glass to hers with a little clang.

"To us," she said tentatively, trying hard to keep her perspective when it would have been so easy for all of this to seem romantic.

They each sipped the golden liquor and then Michael went to what looked like an old, scarred teacher's desk that he used as a kitchen table. He pulled out one of the four mismatched chairs that surrounded it, motioned for her to sit, and took a second chair for himself.

"You must have a lot of details to discuss," Josie said as she joined him.

"A few details and something else," he said mysteriously. Then he launched into the details.

"First of all, here are housekeys," he said, sliding a set from the center of the table to a spot right in front of her. "They're for the front door and the dead bolt, and the gold-colored one works the lock on the back door—although I never use mine and I don't know when you would, either."

"I guess it's good to have one, anyway."

Then he said, "Bathrooms."

"Always a touchy subject," she agreed.

"Since I have one in my bedroom it'll be mine and the one off the upstairs hall can be yours. The downstairs lav, of course, can be used by both of us and by guests, if that's all right with you."

"Sure."

"I won't even go into yours upstairs so feel free

to keep whatever you want in the vanity or the medicine cabinet—I've already cleared them out for you.''

''Thanks.''

''I'm not a stickler when it comes to food. My mother keeps me well stocked with leftovers and casseroles and you're welcome to eat anything that looks good to you. But if you buy yourself something special and don't want me to touch it, just put your name on it and I'll know not to—''

''I'm not a stickler about that, either,'' she said. ''You're welcome to anything I bring in, too.''

He paused before he went on and it let Josie know that the next point wasn't as easy a detail as the others had been.

''I was also thinking that maybe it would be better if we made a rule against bringing dates home,'' he said then, broaching the topic gingerly.

''I hadn't thought about that,'' she said honestly, instantly taking a dislike to the idea that he would be dating at all, let alone that he might bring another woman home. The way he'd brought her home...

Michael smiled again, looking slightly sheepish. ''I don't think I could handle you and some guy...''

Okay, that helped.

''Besides,'' Josie offered, ''we shouldn't run the risk that one of us could have someone here when your mother happened to show up.''

''That, too,'' he agreed. ''Which brings me

neatly to the something else I needed to talk to you about.''

''Does that mean we're done with the details?'' she asked, teasing him slightly.

He smiled a smile that went straight into her bloodstream and made it run quicker.

''Are you making fun of me?''

''Only a little. I didn't know you were a detail man.''

''Really? And I thought you did,'' he countered with a voice full of innuendo.

She knew he'd been referring to the small but important details of making love to her, and she'd walked right into it. But still, just the insinuation was enough to make her think of tiny kisses that had traced the entire outer circles of her ears. About an index finger that had trailed down the inner side of her ankle, along the arch of her foot and around of each of her toes. About the tip of his nose dipping into the hollow of her throat, using her collarbone as a guide to her naked shoulder and the perfect spot for soft kisses…

''Behave yourself,'' she said, unsure whether the warning was more for him or for herself. ''So what's the 'something else' you had to talk to me about?'' she asked to put this conversation more on the up-and-up.

Michael's smile turned into a grin that made her wonder if he somehow knew the path down which her mind had wandered. But he didn't say anything about that. Instead he complied with her demand to know what the something else was. ''I announced our engagement to my mother this morning,'' he said.

''Ah. How did that go over?''

He took another drink of his wine and shrugged before he said, ''She was suspicious at first, but then she warmed to the news. The problem is, she wants us to go to her house for dinner tomorrow night so she can meet you.''

''Why is that a problem?'' Josie asked.

Michael smiled again, dimpling up for her in a way that was like putting a hairdryer to an ice cube when it came to her resolves. ''I was afraid you might have plans or not want to meet her so soon,'' he confessed.

''No, I don't have any plans. And since I'll need to meet your mother sooner or later, it might as well be sooner.''

''So I can let her know we'll be there?'' he said, sounding relieved.

''Sure.''

''Well, you made that easy. Thanks.''

For a moment Michael studied her as if she were too good to be true, and the warmth of those vibrant green eyes was like basking in spring sunshine.

It was also the way he'd looked at her at times over Labor Day weekend.

Just before he'd kissed her.

And once again a rash of memories flooded her mind and tormented her.

Only this time even thinking about toenail clippings wasn't enough to stop it and she knew she had better retreat to the solitude of her own room before the torture got any worse.

"If that's all you wanted to talk about, I should go upstairs and put some of those clothes into the closet so I can get to bed tonight," she said suddenly.

It seemed to surprise him somewhat because his eyebrows arched and pulled together at once, as if he wasn't quite sure what had brought that on. But how could he know, after all, when Josie was likely the only one of them thinking about kissing.

She stood and took her empty glass to the dishwasher before he guessed what was going through her head.

"Yeah, I'd better give my mother a call before I forget about it," he said to her back, sounding a bit baffled.

"I'll let you get to that, then," she said, tapping her thigh twice as a signal to Pip to follow her from the corner where the big dog was lying.

"I probably won't see you again before I go to bed, so good night," she said, when the mastiff was by her side.

"If you need anything—"

"I'll find it," she assured him, calling Pip to follow her and leaving Michael sitting at the kitchen table.

But even as she climbed the stairs to the upper level again she was still thinking about kissing him.

About him kissing her.

And there was one very big problem with that.

She wasn't only thinking about it in the past tense.

Chapter Three

"Manhattan Multiples. Can you hold, please?"

Josie couldn't hear whether the caller had agreed or not but pressed the hold button on the telephone anyway. She had to. In the waiting room directly in front of her reception kiosk, her boss, Eloise Vale had the sound turned up on the television and she was shouting at the screen as if the mayor would stop his press conference to listen to her.

"Stubborn jackass!" Eloise yelled. "Don't you do it, Bill Harper! Don't you say you're cutting us off! I swear, if you do…"

The founder of Manhattan Multiples paused as the mayor announced that in an effort to keep the economy afloat during the current recession he would very likely be ending funding for organizations such as Manhattan Multiples.

"War!" Eloise declared. "This is war now, Harper! I can't believe I nearly married you! I must have been out of my mind! If you think I'll sit still for this, you have another thought coming! Because I won't! I haven't worked this hard, this long, just to let you wipe me out with your stupid bureaucracy!"

By that time the entire staff and several of the clients were rallied behind Eloise and everyone clapped and cheered. Including Josie who not only liked her job and didn't want to leave it just yet, but also believed that Manhattan Multiples provided a valuable service to women who were either pregnant with more than one baby or had just delivered more than one. As well as the families of those women.

Eloise Vale turned off the television and the mayor's press conference with a vengeance and spun around to face the group that had gathered behind her.

"I don't want any of you to worry. I'm going to do my best to make sure our doors stay open. No matter what it takes. I believe in Manhattan Multiples and I won't let it go," she said with conviction before she left the waiting room.

But despite her war cry, Josie still knew her boss was concerned with the future of the place that was as much Eloise's baby as the triplets she'd delivered thirteen years ago.

Manhattan Multiples was a multifaceted center

occupying three floors of a building on Madison Avenue. Eloise had started it as a support group for women having multiple babies, but since its inception in 1995 it had ballooned into a counseling center, numerous support groups, Lamaze training, day care, meditation and yoga classes. All provided invaluable aid and comfort for the additional difficulties and complications of carrying and having more than one baby at a time.

But in the strained economy it was easy to see why funding for such a specialty organization would be the first to go.

Josie suddenly remembered the call she'd put on hold and answered it once again. The woman on the other end needed to enroll in the next session of Lamaze and Josie directed the call to scheduling.

When she hung up, Eloise's assistant Allison Baker joined her in the kiosk and provided her with the opportunity to satisfy some curiosity that had risen during Eloise's tirade at the television.

"I didn't know Eloise nearly married the mayor," Josie whispered.

Allison was a studious sort, far more straitlaced-seeming than Josie, but still they got along well. "I don't know much about it except that she was," Allison confirmed. "It was before she married her late husband."

The husband who had died and left Eloise well off enough to get Manhattan Multiples started but not well off enough to single-handedly keep it going.

"Does the whole almost-marrying-the-mayor history have anything to do with his targeting us in particular for the top of the budget cuts list? Sour grapes, maybe?" Josie asked.

Allison shrugged her shoulders and her eyebrows. "Eloise thinks so. That's what makes it all the worse for her. She feels singled out. As if she's the victim of a vendetta of sorts."

"Apparently it isn't only the fury of scorned women that can be dangerous," Josie paraphrased.

"Apparently," Allison confirmed. "But then relationships are always complicated, aren't they?"

"Oh, boy, are they," Josie agreed a bit too enthusiastically.

Allison looked on the verge of probing that comment but just then Eloise called for her and before she could, she had to leave Josie's kiosk to go back to work.

Of course if Josie had said any more she might have said that complicated seemed like an understatement when it came to her relationship with Michael.

She still wasn't sure she'd done the right thing by agreeing to move in with him. Especially after a night spent lying awake thinking about him being in the room just across the hall. In the bed just across the hall. The bed they'd already shared.

Especially after a night spent lying awake and fighting urges to share that bed again. Urges she didn't want to have. Urges that had left her reconsidering yet again the wisdom of her move and the pretend engagement, and wondering if she should start looking for another place to live first thing this morning.

But about the time her alarm had gone off she'd decided she wasn't going to do that. She'd committed to this peculiar living arrangement and she had to give it a chance. She just didn't like the idea of running from anything.

It was something she took personal pride in. She'd never taken the coward's way out. She'd never shrunk from any problems she had. To her, that was part of being independent and self-sufficient. She dealt with whatever she had to deal with and brought it to as satisfactory a conclusion as she could.

And this was no different.

So she'd sworn to put some concerted effort into making this situation with Michael work. Into quelling these feelings. These inclinations. The whole attraction to Michael. Into conquering it rather than letting it conquer her.

It just wasn't easy.

But it probably wouldn't get any easier—or any less complicated—if she went around blabbing about it to more than Sharon, she decided as she put a folder in the filing cabinet.

No, it was probably good that Allison had been called away before Josie had said more than she had. The fewer people who knew what a weird course she'd just embarked on, the better. Certainly it was better not to let co-workers know what she was doing since they already thought she was a little strange—their resident poet, that's what they called her. Sometimes with a roll of the eyes.

Besides, talking about it wouldn't diffuse the attraction to Michael anyway. And that was her ultimate goal—keeping herself from acting on the urges he inspired and getting over the attraction.

And if she was suffering in the meantime?

She just needed to suffer in silence.

But on the upside, she told herself, angst and emotional upheaval always did give her some good material for poems.

And with as much angst and upheaval as she'd experienced just since moving into Michael's place the night before she ought to come out of this with an entire collection.

"Wow, look at you! This is only dinner at my mother's, you know. You didn't have to go all-out. Although you do look incredible," Michael said when Josie came down the stairs to the living room that evening.

She held her arms out to her sides and twirled so the filmy, African-print, ankle-length skirt she wore spread out around her. "This old thing?" she said, making a joke of it.

But in truth she'd spent a full hour choosing something to wear tonight. Of course she'd told herself that she was paying so much attention to her appearance because she was about to meet her pretend future mother-in-law and she wanted the other woman to approve of her.

It was just that that had a small hole shot

through it when she'd opted for the slightly sexy, cream-colored lace camisole as a top. And then dusted her shoulders with the glittery powder she usually reserved for clubbing. And applied an artfully seductive hint of eye shadow, mascara and blush. Not to mention the splash of perfume.

None of those were likely to make her seem like the demure daughter-in-law she assumed a mother would want for her son.

But it was too late now to tone herself down—unless she removed the hoop earrings or the twelve thin strands of beads that wrapped her right wrist. Which she had no intention of doing.

What she did do, though, was cover her shoulders in the shawl she'd chosen to add some propriety as she took in the sight of Michael.

"It doesn't look to me like I overdressed," she said then, noting the dark gray slacks and dove gray polo shirt he'd changed into just since she'd arrived home from work. "You're clean-shaven, you smell incredible, and you look pretty darn good yourself," she said matter-of-factly. "Something tells me this is not how you would usually go to Mom's for an ordinary, everyday weeknight dinner."

He grinned for her but was nonplussed. "It isn't just an ordinary, everyday weeknight dinner. It's the dinner I'm bringing my new fiancée to so she can meet my mother. I thought gym shorts and a sweaty T-shirt were probably not a great idea."

Although she had no doubt he would have

looked terrific in those, too. Especially since they'd show more skin.

But she didn't say that.

Instead she said, ''That was my thinking, too. That I should dress up for the meet-the-mom dinner.'' Liar, liar, liar...

''Great minds work alike,'' Michael agreed. Then he checked his watch. ''We should probably get going. Being late would get us off on the wrong foot with my mother.''

''We don't want to do that,'' Josie agreed.

She turned her attention to Pip then, warning him to be a good boy and turning on the radio for him. ''For company,'' she informed Michael as she did.

Pip followed them to the front door where Josie gave him a bone and then she and Michael left.

The wind was blowing so Michael suggested they drive the short distance they might have otherwise walked.

His red two-seater sports car was parked three doors down and when they reached it he held open Josie's door for her before he rounded the rear of the vehicle and got behind the wheel.

On the way to his mother's house he used the opportunity to point out to Josie where the neighborhood dry cleaner, coffee shop, news stand and food market were. And then they were pulling up in front of a brownstone similar to Michael's place except his mother's had shutters bordering all the windows.

''Does your mother live here alone?'' Josie

asked when Michael had parked and come around again to open her door for her.

"No, my younger sister Cindy still lives at home. She'll be here tonight, too."

Michael waited for Josie to go up the steps ahead of him and when he'd joined her on the landing at the front door he leaned over to say into her ear, "Whatever you do, don't agree to let my mother take you to her hairdresser to have your hair done."

Josie's hand went automatically to her short bob, smoothing one side behind her ear self-consciously. "Is there something wrong with my hair?"

"It's perfect just the way it is. But unless it's four inches from your head, my mother will try to get you to see her girl."

"Have *you* seen her girl?" Josie asked with heavy insinuation.

"Seen, as in dated?" he qualified.

Josie confirmed the query with raised eyebrows.

Michael chuckled wryly. "I've dated almost every female who has ever crossed my mother's path. You don't think I came lightly to the point of pretending to be engaged, do you?"

"I suppose not."

"Just don't let her talk you into a beauty day with her."

"Okay," Josie agreed. "Anything else I should be warned of?"

"Too many things to go into. You're just going to have to fly by the seat of your pants," he said as he reached in front of her and opened the door, allowing her a whiff of that clean-scented after-shave.

"We're here, Ma," he called as he motioned for Josie to go inside and followed her there, too.

"Kitchen," a woman's voice called from the rear of the place that was so overfurnished and overdecorated with so many mismatched items it looked like a garage sale waiting to happen.

Michael pointed in the direction he wanted Josie to go. But he must have noticed her taking in the clutter because he bent to her ear a second time and said, "She won't throw out *anything*."

That explained the eclectic collection, thought Josie. She merely nodded her understanding as they passed through the arch that led to the dining room—where the table was already set—and arrived at the kitchen.

"Hi," a woman just closing the refrigerator greeted them.

"Hey, Cin," Michael answered her.

But before he could introduce the tall, thin, pale-complexioned replica of himself who had to be his sister, the other woman in the kitchen spun around from the sink and said, "Oh, no, me first. Mother of the groom comes before sister of the groom."

The older woman seemed to charge Josie then and the younger stepped aside timidly to let her by.

"Hi, Ma," Michael said to his mother, planting a perfunctory kiss on her cheek as she wiped her hands on a dish towel and took a long look at Josie from head to toe as Michael did the honors.

"Elsa Dunnigan, this is Josie Tate, my fiancée."

"Finally!" Elsa exclaimed as if that announcement had been forever in coming. "And you're so pretty. No wonder he turned his nose up at everybody I sent him out with—you put them all to shame."

"Oh, I don't know about that," Josie said, embarrassed but pleased just the same.

Michael nodded toward his sister. "And this is Cindy, my sister. Cindy, Josie."

"Nice to meet you," Josie said.

Cindy opened her mouth to respond but before she managed it, her mother broke in.

"Josie—is your name really Josephine?"

"No, just Josie."

"Well, welcome to the family, Josie. I can't tell you how happy I am to be able to say that."

"Yeah, now you can devote all your time to finding Cindy a husband," Michael said wryly, casting a teasing glance at his sister.

"Thanks," Cindy said almost in an aside. "As if going out with everyone from the mailman to the mortician who did Aunt Fiona's funeral hasn't been enough."

"Maybe Josie knows a nice man for you," Elsa Dunnigan said, completely ignoring the lack of enthusiasm on her daughter's part. Then, to Josie, she said, "Or maybe you have a brother or a cousin…"

"Sorry," Josie answered, finding the exchange—and Michael's mother—amusing. "I don't have any family at all."

"But you'll keep your eyes open," Elsa commanded just before she herded everyone into the dining room for dinner.

Conversation over pot roast, potatoes, carrots, salad and rolls was pleasant, superficial and guided by Elsa who seemed never at a loss for words. She asked Josie a question here and there about herself but the answers didn't seem to really register as Elsa hurried on to other subjects as if they were important pieces of information that she might forget to pass on if she didn't do it immediately.

Since most of what Elsa said was about people or places Josie didn't know, it left her free to surreptitiously study the older woman.

There was no doubt Elsa was Michael's mother. They shared the same eyes, the same facial structure, the same hair color—although seeing the large bouffant flip the older woman's hair was teased into gave Josie a belated understanding of why Michael had advised her not to let his mother talk her into going to her beautician.

But on the whole, Elsa was an attractive woman. She was trim and energetic and she had lovely skin that was only beginning to wrinkle slightly around the eyes.

She was also a good cook and Josie told her so.

"Don't worry, I'll teach you all of Michael's favorite dishes," she promised.

Then she got down to business.

"So, what's the wedding date?" Elsa asked as

they all pitched in to clear the table when they'd finished eating.

"Ma," Michael said in a warning tone. "I told you we were having a long engagement."

"It takes forever to plan a wedding. We can't start too soon," Elsa said, ignoring her son's response.

"It's too far off to even start thinking about," Michael persisted.

"What do you think, Josie?" Elsa said, as if enlisting an ally. "Couldn't we at least set a date? Even if it's a year away?"

"It's probably more than a year away," Michael said before Josie could answer for herself. "We want to get to know each other, remember?"

"You won't know each other in a year? How long does it take?"

"As long as we want."

"I still haven't heard Josie say that she wants to wait," Elsa persisted.

"I do," Josie said in a hurry to get it in.

Not that it mattered because Elsa waved that away as if she were swatting at a fly. "You'll change your mind. Michael said you work at that Manhattan Multiples place that's been in the newspapers lately. Being around so many pregnant women and beautiful babies—you'll want that for yourself. Mark my words."

"I don't think where I work is going to influence that," Josie hedged.

"You're wrong. Now that you know the man you're going to marry, you'll just want to get on with it. Why wait? You love each other. You're engaged. Living together. What's to wait for?'' Elsa reasoned.

They were all in the kitchen again and Josie was near enough to Michael and Cindy to hear Cindy goad her brother under her breath, ''Looks like you're still first priority. Now it's just for setting a wedding date and having kids rather than finding a wife.''

Michael made a face at her that Josie thought was probably a holdover from childhood.

Then, to get even, he said to their mother, ''You've already gotten me engaged, Ma, now it's Cindy's turn. Give me a break and find her a fiancé, then Josie and I will talk about setting a date.''

Cindy wrinkled her nose at her brother and threw a hot pad at him.

But Elsa ignored them and continued to press Josie. ''Let's just set a general date—like June of next year—so I'll have something to tell my friends.''

''It's enough to tell your friends that I'm engaged, Ma. You don't have to tell them more than that,'' Michael interjected for Josie.

''But they'll ask and ask, and I have to be able to say something,'' Elsa insisted.

''Say that we're having a long engagement,'' he suggested, coming full circle once more.

Then he winked at Josie and smiled a smile that seemed to wrap around her as if they really were a couple sharing a private glance.

And for a third time he leaned over to her ear, whispering in a warm, intimate breath of air, "Are you sorry you said yes yet?"

Josie just laughed.

But surprisingly she wasn't sorry at all. In fact, as she took in the sight of the small family working together to clear the dinner mess, as she watched the dynamics of their relationship, the closeness and affection they shared even as they good-naturedly bickered, she realized that she was enjoying herself. Enjoying them and being a part of it all. More than they knew. More than she might have guessed she would.

Although, as Elsa Dunnigan continued to press both Josie and Michael, Josie thought she'd better find a way to distract the elder woman before Elsa did just what Sharon had warned and steamrolled a wedding date out of her.

So Josie changed the subject, pretending a deep and abiding desire to know what Michael's favorite foods were and how to prepare them.

Just like any good fiancée.

It was late by the time Josie and Michael got away from his mother and back home again. Pip had been alone for a long while and even though having the small yard freed Josie of the need to walk the dog, Pip wanted some attention.

Knowing he wouldn't leave her alone until she played with him, Josie kneeled on the living room floor and said, "Get your tug."

The bull mastiff promptly went to the bucket of

dog toys Michael hadn't minded being left in the corner of the room. Pip dug through them and then loped back to Josie with a heavy-duty rope fashioned in a figure eight.

Josie grabbed one of the loops, Pip clamped his massive jaws around the other, and the war was on as Michael stood by and watched.

"So how did I do?" Josie asked amid nearly having her arm pulled out of the socket by Pip's battle.

"Tonight with my mother?" Michael asked to clarify.

"Mmm-hmm," she confirmed a bit disjointedly because Pip jerked her so hard it nearly gave her whiplash.

That made Michael laugh but ask with concern, "Are you okay?"

"I'm used to it," Josie assured with a laugh of her own that allowed Michael to return to the previous subject.

"You did great tonight, I'm just sorry you didn't get more than two words in edgewise," he said.

Josie's laugh this time was wry. "Nobody but your mom got in two words edgewise," she pointed out.

"I was kind of hoping you might, though. So I'd get the answers to some of the questions my mother asked you. But that never seemed to happen."

"What did you want to know?"

Pip gave a tug so fierce Josie lost her grip of the opposite end of the rope and Michael lunged for her as if he thought she was going to end up on her face.

She didn't and he stopped short of actually touching her. Which caused a wave of disappointment Josie silently chastised herself for.

"Come here, Pip," Michael commanded then, clearly to spare Josie any more of the abuse.

Pip was eager for a greater challenge and did as he was told, taking the toy to Michael, who played the same game only with enough strength to make it more worthwhile for the big dog.

As he did, he said, "It just occurred to me that if we're going to keep up the appearance of an engaged couple getting to know each other, maybe we need to get to know each other. Some, anyway."

"That makes sense," Josie agreed.

Michael sat on the edge of the sofa, handling Pip's best pulls as if they were nothing at all for him when similar force from the mastiff would have dragged Josie across the room.

She'd remained where she was on the floor and she couldn't help taking in—and appreciating—the sight of his biceps bulging against his shirtsleeves, of his thighs testing the strength of the legs of his pants.

But she tried to keep herself focused on what they were talking about anyway. "What did your mother ask that you wanted to hear the answer to?"

"For instance, there was the question about

whether you had a brother to fix up with my sister—no brothers, no cousins, no family at all?''

''None,'' she confirmed.

''How come?''

''My parents were both 'only' children and they didn't marry until they were older. Their own parents had passed away before I was born. And I was an only child. So there was just my folks and me. And they were killed when I was eight.''

Michael's brow furrowed into deep creases. ''How were they killed?''

''They were thrill-seekers—that's what they said about themselves. Mountain climbing. Bungee jumping. Parachuting out of planes. Hot-air balloon racing. You name it, they did it. When I was eight they were killed in a climbing accident in the Himalayas. Over Labor Day weekend, as a matter of fact.''

''I'm sorry,'' he said, sounding as if he meant it.

''Me, too.'' Sorry enough to still get into a dark funk this past Labor Day weekend and do something crazy like spend three days in bed with a man she didn't know...

''Who raised you if there were no grandparents or aunts or uncles?'' Michael asked then.

''The nuns of the Little Sisters of the Poor orphanage. In Denver, Colorado—we'd lived in several different states before that but that's where I was at the time of the accident so that's where I ended up.''

''You grew up in an orphanage? I didn't know

those things existed anymore. I thought the foster care system had replaced them.''

''I think for the most part it has. But the baby-sitter they'd hired for me that weekend was a nun affiliated with the orphanage, so that's where she took me. The courts decided that might as well be where I stayed. Until I was eighteen and graduated from high school.''

Michael shook his head as if he could hardly believe what he was hearing. ''Wow. That must have been strange.''

''It was at first. I'd lost my parents. My home. All I had was a bed in a ward with seven other girls and nothing but a nightstand and a trunk at the foot of the bed for my stuff. But eventually I got used to it and after living there a long time…'' Josie shrugged. ''I don't know. I guess anywhere you live becomes home.''

''It sounds so impersonal. So institutional. And cold.''

''It wasn't *that* bad. It was like what I imagine boarding school is. Only I didn't get to go home for holidays or vacations. But for the most part the nuns were warm, kind, loving people who did their best.''

''With how many kids at a time?''

''It varied over the years. Babies were usually adopted out pretty quick but those of us who had come in older weren't so lucky, and the nuns also took in some teenagers, some who were runaways. But maximum capacity was seventy kids.''

''*Seventy* kids? For how much staff?''

"Around a dozen, usually."

"That's not a great ratio. I'm surprised they even knew who you were."

Josie laughed at that, too. "There wasn't a lot of one-on-one, parent-child kind of attention, no. There just wasn't that much to go around. But they all did know my name."

"This breaks my heart, Josie," Michael said as if it really did.

Josie laughed yet again. "I told you, it wasn't that bad. I did all right. I'm here, aren't I? And none the worse for wear."

He could control Pip with one hand and still study Josie with eyes that warmed her to the core in spite of the subject they were discussing.

"You know," he said, "at the end of that unmentionable weekend we spent together, when we agreed neither of us wanted a serious involvement, you said you didn't like attachments. Now, knowing this, that kind of surprises me."

"Why?"

"It just seems like one of the things you'd want the most after growing up like that is a home and a family of your own."

"Why?" she repeated.

"I would just think that you'd want to put down roots. Have some close relationships—home and family."

"It's just the opposite, actually. I learned at an early age *not* to get too attached to people. That they can be here today, gone tomorrow. Gone *for-*

ever. Besides, I like being on my own. Being *un-*attached.''

''You're pretty attached to Pip, here,'' Michael pointed out as if to find a chink in her armor. ''You were willing to be kicked out of your apartment for him.''

''I'm *responsible* for Pip. I found him in the street and took him in when I could have just turned him over to the pound. Since I kept him, he's mine to take care of even if that means we get kicked out of an apartment. But I knew from the get-go that he won't be around forever. That I'll outlive him. So there's no illusion that I'll never be without him.''

''But you *are* attached to him and it'll hurt when you lose him.''

''It'll hurt, but my life will go on just the same. It won't really be changed.''

''The way it would if you had a husband and kids one minute and not the next?''

''Exactly.''

Michael didn't look as if he believed she would be able to take losing even Pip so much in stride. But he didn't say that. Instead, as Pip seemed to grow weary of the tug game, he pulled the big dog to his side and began to pet him with calming strokes of those big hands.

''What about my mother's theory that working where you do will make you want to have a baby of your own? You really must think that's not true, then.''

''Definitely not true. Not that I don't like kids—

I do. And babies—I always did after-school duty in the nursery at the orphanage. And I like my job, too. But that's all it is—a job just like a lot of other jobs I've had. Something to pay the bills and keep me in paper and pens to write poems with. When I get tired of Manhattan Multiples, I'll move on. And in the meantime, just working there isn't likely to make me want babies of my own.''

''You don't like to get attached to jobs, either?'' he said, referring back to her comment that when she tired of Manhattan Multiples she'd move on.

''No, I don't. I don't like to get too rooted in anything. Except my writing.''

''Which you can bring with you anywhere and can never be taken away from you.''

''Mmm.''

''So how many jobs have you had?'' he asked.

''A lot. I've waited tables, arranged flowers, delivered pizzas, done telephone sales, clerked in department stores, stacked grocery store shelves, groomed dogs, been a dental assistant, cleaned houses and offices, I even worked construction one summer.''

That made him smile again. ''Construction?''

''Complete with hard hat. Being a poet doesn't pay too well, in case you didn't know.''

''I can just see you, sitting on a high beam writing verse at lunchtime.''

''The muse isn't particular about the where or the when.''

''Have you made money writing?'' he asked then.

"A little here and there. I've won a few cash prizes and I've had some things published in anthologies and magazines. But not enough to live off."

"Is that your ultimate goal? To make your living writing poetry?"

"To be Maya Angelou? I would love that. But it's a little unlikely."

"And the struggle doesn't wear you out? I mean, working a million jobs to support yourself when what you really want to do is write?"

"Sure, it gets me down sometimes. But every job is a new experience and that's great grist for the mill."

"And you never get tired of the job changing and think you'll just chuck the poetry, settle on one career and devote yourself to it?"

Josie pulled back as if in horror. "In the first place, I love the writing too much to ever give it up. And it wouldn't let me even if I tried. The words, the ideas, are just there, in my head, whether I like it or not, whether I want them to be there or not. I have to do something with them. But in the second place, settling into one career and devoting myself to it just sounds so restrictive!"

"Okay, okay, I get the point," Michael said with another laugh. "Josie Tate has to be free. No attachments. No long-term commitments. Just you and your dog, going wherever the wind blows. Writing poetry along the way."

It was Josie's turn to laugh because he made that

sound so silly. "Hey, count your blessings that I'm a little unorthodox. Who else would come in here and pretend to be your fiancée to get you off the hook with your mother?"

"Too true," he conceded.

He was still petting Pip in long, slow strokes that went from the top of the dog's head down his back. And even though Josie had been trying not to watch, her gaze went there on its own now.

Long, slow strokes of Michael's big, strong hand...

"I think I'd better call it a night," she said suddenly, almost frantically since she'd just realized that she was actually feeling envious of her dog.

Michael didn't say anything to stop her as she got to her feet. In fact he gave Pip a final roughing up behind the ears, patted his head and stood himself. "Yeah, I'm ready to go up, too."

Josie had been hoping he'd stay downstairs, that she could just say a quick good-night and leave him there. She thought maybe she'd have better luck falling asleep if she knew there was more distance between them than the hallway that separated their rooms.

But Michael locked the front door and turned out the lights, following Josie and Pip as they headed up the steps.

"I'm on duty tomorrow," he said from behind her. "Seven a.m. tomorrow to 7:00 a.m. Wednesday. So I'll probably be out of here before you're up and home but in bed the morning after."

That should help at least the next night. A little. If only she could get through tonight.

"Is there anything I need to know about things around here while you're gone?" she asked as they reached their facing bedroom doors.

"Nothing I can think of. But the number for the station house is on the back of the calendar beside the phone if you need to get hold of me."

Just the mention of getting hold of him only exacerbated the thoughts and inclinations running through her in regard to this man who stood only inches away from her—tall and staggeringly handsome and so sexy it seemed to radiate from him.

"I'm sure I won't need to," she said as if she were determined not to need anything of him.

"Well, if you do, it's okay. It rings in on a line that doesn't tie up in-coming emergency calls."

Josie nodded. "Good to know."

"And if my mother bothers you—I know she made you give her your work phone number—you can call and tell me and I'll deal with her."

Was he stalling? Or did it just seem as if he was looking for anything to talk about to keep this going?

"I'm sure it'll be all right even if she does call me. Don't worry about it."

"I'm just saying—"

"I know. And I appreciate it. If she starts bugging me at work and it gets out of hand, I'll let you know."

"Good."

He was staring at her very intently. His vibrant

green eyes seemed to search hers and she wondered if there was something else—something more important—that he wanted to say.

Except that he didn't say anything. He just held her eyes with his. And the longer it went on, the more Josie began to wonder if talking wasn't at all what was on his mind. If he might be considering something more physical.

"We should probably both get to bed, then," she said, fully intending it to put an end to this evening. But something about the way she said it had caused it to sound more insinuative. As if they should go to bed together...

"I mean, you know, get to sleep. Alone. In our own separate rooms," she amended, regretting it the minute the words came out because they'd made a bigger deal than was warranted of what she'd said the first time.

Michael smiled a mischievous smile. "Yeah, we probably should get some sleep," he agreed, his tone at once full of innuendo and teasing.

He reached a single index finger to her hair, putting it behind her ear the way she so often did, and leaving her skin tingling in his wake. "Thanks for tonight and putting up with my mother."

"It was nothing," she assured him, wishing her voice hadn't sounded so soft and breathy.

"It was something to me."

Still he didn't move toward his door. He stayed there in the hall, nearer, it seemed, than a moment before, looking down into her eyes.

And Josie seriously thought he was going to kiss

her. Seriously enough that she was debating with herself whether or not she was going to let him.

Or if she was capable of denying herself what she suddenly wanted more than she should.

But the debate was for nothing because a moment later Michael broke the gaze that had tied them together and took a step backward, away from her.

"I'll see you on Wednesday," he said then.

Josie mentally leaped back into reality, as if she hadn't been mesmerized by him the split second before, and said, "I'll be quiet when I get up that morning so I don't wake you."

"Okay, but a little noise isn't a problem. Once I'm down for the count I can sleep through an earthquake."

Josie merely nodded, thinking that that hadn't been her experience with him before. Over Labor Day weekend the slightest movement on her part had roused him. And aroused him...

But she didn't remind him of that. She didn't want to remember it herself.

Instead she said, "Good night, then."

"'Night," he answered.

But he still didn't go into his room and she wasn't sure why.

She was sure, though, that if she didn't go into hers, she was apt to do something she'd regret.

So she crossed the threshold into her bedroom, where Pip had already curled himself onto his doggy bed, and closed the door on Michael.

Michael whose image she took with her.

All the way with her to wash her face, to put on her pajamas. All the way into bed with her.

Where she gave up hope of a restful night's sleep when she closed her eyes and found him so vividly there in her mind.

Gorgeous.

Sexy as all get-out.

And making her want that kiss she thought they'd almost had in the hall....

Chapter Four

The telephone was ringing when Josie arrived at Manhattan Multiples on Wednesday morning. She was an hour early and the first one in. Had she let the phone ring two more times, the answering service would have picked up. But out of reflex she'd grabbed the receiver before it rang into the service.

"Manhattan Multiples."

"Get Eloise Vale on the phone."

The caller was male and angry, but Josie kept cool. "I'm sorry. I'm afraid we don't open until nine and Eloise Vale isn't in yet. May I take a message?"

"You can tell her Bill Harper—"

"Excuse me, Bill Harper the Mayor?"

"Yes, Bill Harper the Mayor—"

"In person? Or are you his assistant or something?"

"This is Bill Harper. *I'm* Bill Harper," he said, clearly forcing patience.

"Oh."

"Can you take a message or not?" he demanded.

"I'd be happy to, Mr. Mayor."

"Good. You can tell her that there is nothing personal in my decision to make budget cuts for funding to nonprofit organizations like Manhattan Multiples. Nor is Manhattan Multiples at the *top* of the list, it is merely *on* the list. And I don't appreciate her releasing that statement to the press accusing me of having a personal vendetta against her because she married Walter Vale rather than me. In the first place, that's the most absurd thing I've ever heard. In the second place, I would never use the office of mayor to revenge some sort of long-ago slight suffered in my personal life. And furthermore, if Eloise wants to discuss the history we have together she can do it with me directly, not in a public forum. Have you got all that?"

"Yes, sir," Josie assured her, a bit stunned to have been the recipient of the tirade.

"Good. Make sure *Mrs.* Vale gets the message."

"Yes, sir," Josie repeated.

"Thank you," he finished and hung up.

"I guess this really is war," Josie muttered to herself as she replaced the receiver in its cradle.

Eloise came in just then and instead of greeting

her boss, Josie said, "You just missed a call from the mayor."

"No?" The forty-two-year-old widow with the omniscient gray eyes responded in disbelief.

"Oh, yes," Josie said. "But you ought to be glad."

"He's mad," Eloise guessed, sounding pleased by it.

"Hopping mad. Yelling mad." Much the way Eloise had been when she'd watched Bill Harper's press conference announcing the budget cuts that could well cost Manhattan Multiples its funding.

"What did he say?" the pretty ash-blonde asked.

Josie repeated the diatribe in its entirety since it was fresh enough in her mind not to have forgotten a word of it.

When she'd finished, Eloise said, "Oh, he'd like that, wouldn't he? For me to keep my mouth shut in public but talk to him in private? He didn't call me personally to tell me he was taking away my money, did he? No, it was all right for *him* to announce it to the press. But I'm supposed to just take it lying down? I'm supposed to call him to *discuss* it so the people who elected him don't know he's using the power of his office to avenge a broken heart? Well, think again, Bill Harper!"

Eloise was at full steam by the time she'd reached the end of her harangue. But rather than infuriate her the way the mayor's original announcement had, his reaction to her rebuttal seemed to have invigorated her.

"You definitely got a rise out of him," Josie said.

"Score one for our side!" Eloise exclaimed.

Then, as if it had just registered that Josie was there, the older woman said, "What are you doing in here so early?"

"Oh. Uh…I was supposed to have breakfast with a friend but she slept through her alarm and didn't show up. Since I was already downstairs at the coffee shop when she called to tell me she wasn't going to make it, I just came on up."

Josie wasn't a very smooth liar and Eloise looked as if she didn't quite believe her. But she didn't press it. And Josie was quick to change the subject back to the one that was more likely to enthrall her boss.

"Do you want me to get the mayor on the phone for you?"

"I don't think so. Let's let him stew awhile," Eloise decided.

To Josie's relief the distraction worked because Eloise didn't say any more about Josie being early and simply went into her own office.

Josie hadn't wanted to lie to Eloise, who was one of the nicest, most caring and nurturing people Josie had ever met. But she could hardly have told her the truth about why she was in the office before she needed to be. She could hardly tell her that she'd had to get out of the house before she did something stupid.

Something even more stupid than the way she'd spent the night before.

Not that she'd intended to do anything stupid with her time alone in the house while Michael did his twenty-four-hour shift at the fire station. On the contrary, she'd hoped to use those hours alone to get some control over her attraction to him. To shore up her defenses to the effects he had on her. To gain some perspective. To strengthen her resolves so she could be impervious to him when she saw him again.

But had she done any of that?

Not by a long shot.

In fact, she'd done the opposite.

It was just that it was harder than she'd thought because even though Michael himself hadn't been in the house, it was still *his* house. His house where they'd spent a concentrated weekend together. His house filled with his things.

Like the stair banister he'd slid down exuberantly at three o'clock Saturday morning so he could catch her at the bottom and keep her from leaving after the first time they'd made love.

Like the refrigerator where he'd stood in the lee of the open door in nothing but his shorts, his incredibly muscular, carved body bathed in only the golden light as he looked for sustenance after the second time he'd made love to her.

Like the sofa he'd thrown himself on to show her just how exhausted he was that Sunday night over Labor Day weekend after more times making love than either of them had been able to keep track of.

Plus, to top it all off, there was his bedroom.

The bedroom she'd become so familiar with during the three days she'd spent in it.

The bedroom that had seemed to call to her late the night before in the midst of her sleepless wanderings.

She hadn't gone all the way into it but she had opened the door and stood in the doorway. Just looking. Just remembering. Just drinking in the lingering scent of his aftershave wafting out to her.

She'd stared in at his big bed with its cocoa-colored quilt and flashed back to all they'd done there over the Labor Day weekend, fighting the urge to actually go to that bed. To lie down on it. To close her eyes and mentally relive every moment of that weekend. Every stroke of Michael's hands. Every kiss. Every thrust of him inside her...

No, in the end she most certainly had not succeeded in gaining any control, any perspective. Nor were her defenses shored up.

However, her resolve to find a way to escape any more self-torture over Michael Dunnigan was even stronger.

Which was why, when she'd heard him come in this morning and she'd wanted badly to see him, to hear his voice, she'd instead rushed through her shower, thrown on her clothes and charged out of the house before she actually did set eyes on him.

Putting her at work an hour early.

But certainly she couldn't tell all of that to Eloise.

No, this was her problem and she had to deal

with it. On her own. In any way she could. No matter what it took.

Until her attraction to Michael just wore itself out and she could look at him, be around him—or be without him—and be totally unaffected.

That was her goal. And she was going to reach it.

Even if it killed her.

And it just might, she thought.

Because it was as if the man had seeped into her pores and become a part of her.

A part she couldn't seem to shake.

Michael wasn't at the house when Josie got home at the end of the day, but he'd left her a note saying he'd gone to run some errands.

She thought that was considerate of him.

She also had to fight the letdown feeling that overcame her when she realized she still wasn't going to see him.

But it was for the best, she reminded herself. It was just what she wanted, what she needed. It served the same purpose as her leaving early for work because it meant that it was possible their paths might not cross at all today or tonight, either. Then tomorrow morning he'd be gone on another twenty-four-hour shift at the firehouse so she definitely wouldn't see him. And the more time they *didn't* spend together, the better.

So what if she felt letdown? she asked herself as she changed out of her work clothes and into a pair of gray hip-hugger slacks and a snug, lighter gray crew-neck T-shirt. Feeling letdown was not a crisis. She'd get over it. And when she got over having feelings like that altogether, she'd also be over this attraction to Michael. And that was what she was aiming for.

Once she was dressed, she played with Pip for a while before she fed the big dog. Then she answered Michael's consideration in kind by leaving him a note, telling him where she was, and headed for the Underground Café.

The Underground Café was the coffee shop on the corner. Michael had pointed it out to her on their way to his mother's place on Monday night and, on Tuesday, on her way home from work, Josie had stopped in.

Over a mocha latte she'd discovered that Wednesday was open-mike night for folk music. She'd talked to the manager, convinced him that a poetry reading would fit in, and he'd agreed to put her name on the list for this evening. One poem. Not too long. Just before intermission. That was the deal.

The café was almost completely full when Josie arrived there. She snagged a tiny corner table for herself, ordered a chai tea and settled in as the manager welcomed everyone and introduced a duo—two men, both with guitars—to kick off the evening.

They weren't half bad at what they'd informed the audience was a Greek folk ballad. As Josie enjoyed the music she surveyed the crowd she'd be reciting to.

There were all ages, all races, and a fairly even spread of men and women. The attire ran the gamut from work suits to one guy in wooden clogs and a woman wearing an elaborate, African turban-type headgear, wider than her shoulders, with several long scarves hanging from it.

Josie had learned long ago that diversity and open-mindedness was a good thing when it came to poetry, so she was glad not to be facing an entire contingent of stuffed shirts.

At not quite ten o'clock the manager stepped up to the microphone and said, "We're doing something a little different tonight."

He went on to good-naturedly explain that Josie had twisted his arm and would be sharing with them a poem she'd written.

There wasn't a lot of gleeful hooting and hollering in response to that announcement, but there weren't any boos, either. The audience and some of the other performers merely clapped, and Josie took that as encouragement enough as she went up to the mike beside the café door.

"Hi," she said, glancing around to include the entire roomful of people. "This poem is called 'Contribution' and it's short, so if you're hating the interruption in the music, don't worry, this won't take long."

That elicited some laughter and it helped Josie relax.

Until the café door opened and in walked Michael.

He was dressed simply, in jeans and an Irishgreen polo shirt. But one look in her direction, one wave of a big hand, and something in the pit of her stomach began to flutter.

She had no choice but to ignore it, acknowledging the wave only with a slight raise of her chin before she forced her concentration back to her poem, struggling suddenly to remember it.

"'Contribution'," she repeated.

"We dream for all now.
That is what we have left.
We travel, a naked foot
On a path of glass.
We watch, and wait.
The last drop of rain
Hanging off the tip
Of a leaf.
We dream for us.
That is what we have left.
A careful fire,
Slowly grows—
For all now."

When she finished she paused for a moment for effect, then said, "See? That wasn't too painful, was it?"

Another laugh preceded applause—much of it enthusiastic.

From her corner table, Michael was the most enthusiastic of all. He even whistled. And although Josie appreciated the support, it was slightly embarrassing.

"Thank you," she said into the microphone to the room in general. She then turned the mike over to the manager again, who announced a fifteen-minute break before the next singer as Josie returned to her table.

When she got there Michael did a second round of nearly silent clapping for her benefit alone.

Wrapping an arm around her middle, Josie did an exaggerated, courtly bow. Then she straightened and said, "Hi."

"Nice. Very nice," Michael responded, nodding in the direction of the microphone to let her know he was referring to her poem.

"Thanks."

The table was tall and round, the chairs necessarily tall, too. And awkward for someone as short as Josie to climb onto. When she did, she accidentally brushed Michael's knee with her own.

Just that simple contact sent little tingles up her thigh but she tried not to think about it and said, "I didn't expect to see you here."

He shrugged one broad shoulder. "I finished all the stuff I had to do, went home and found your note. I wanted to hear your poem," he said simply enough.

"Does that mean you're a fan?" she joked.

"Absolutely. I've been hooked since the very first time I heard you," he said, making it sound like there had been many occasions since.

"You've only heard me once," she pointed out. "Although, coming to hear me a second time—on purpose—might make you my biggest fan."

"No doubt about that," he said with a tone full of insinuation.

Josie ignored it and instead, like a schoolteacher quizzing an ornery kid, she said, "And what did you think of this particular selection?"

"I liked it. I didn't understand it, but I liked it," he added with a grin.

Josie laughed. "Do you want me to explain it to you?"

"Because I'm a big dumb lug who can't figure it out for himself?"

Michael, a big dumb lug? Not by any stretch of the imagination.

"Yes," she said with a grin of her own to let him know she was teasing.

"Watch yourself. I was going to walk you home but if you don't behave I'll leave you to the wolves."

Josie liked the idea that he'd come especially to hear her work and to walk her home, but she wasn't going to let him know that. It wasn't even something she should be pleased by. She just couldn't seem to help it.

One of the waitresses appeared tableside to ask if she could get Michael something and to refill Josie's chai.

They both declined.

"You don't even want a cup of coffee?" Josie asked when the waitress had left again.

"No. I just came for you."

That only intensified the flutters and tingles he'd already set off in her.

"Well, in that case, I was going to leave after my turn at the mike. Work, tomorrow, you know?"

"Then I got here just in time," he said, getting up from his chair and holding the back of Josie's steady as she climbed down.

They bickered a bit because Michael insisted on leaving the tip for the chai she'd already paid for. But he won through pure brute strength—he left the bills on the table and took her elbow to steer her out of the place before she could do anything about it.

Of course he had an unfair advantage because the touch of his hand on her arm not only caught her off guard, it sent her stomach into still more flutters and her skin into still more tingles. By the time she had herself under control, Michael had already ushered her out of the café and onto the sidewalk that ran in front of it.

"What a beautiful night," Josie said once they were there.

It was the perfect temperature—not too hot, not too cool. The air was still. The moon was full in a cloudless sky littered with stars. And a few early autumn leaves drifted down from the branches of the elm, oak and maple trees that lined the street.

"Want to take the long way home?" Michael offered.

"Sure."

"Then I can show you where the deli is."

"And here I thought you just wanted to draw out your time with me."

He merely smiled at that, pointed in the direction they should go and waited for Josie to start out.

"So how did you do in your new digs while I was at work?" he asked as they set off at a leisurely pace. "Did you miss me?"

"Horribly," she answered, making the truth sound like a lie. "But other than that, no one broke in to steal the family jewels or ravage my body."

"I had the only family jewels I own with me and not breaking in to ravage your body *had* to be an oversight."

Josie laughed but chastised anyway. "*Now* who isn't behaving?"

"Sorry," he said unapologetically.

"How was work?" Josie countered. "Did *you* miss *me?*"

"I did," he answered as if he genuinely had. "You were on my mind the whole time and it cost me a lot of money."

"Why is that?"

"We played poker until nearly four this morning and since I kept thinking about you instead of my cards I lost more hands than I won."

"What were you thinking about?"

Too flirty. She wished it had come out more matter-of-factly. Or that she hadn't said it at all.

"Just things," Michael said intriguingly.

"Good things? Bad things? Things like breaking our engagement and kicking me out of the house…"

He frowned down at her. "Why would I break our engagement and kick you out of the house?"

"Oh, I don't know. Maybe it's just too complicated or uncomfortable or difficult?"

"Is that what you were thinking about all night?" he asked.

"No," she said feebly.

Michael wasn't fooled. "I went to work and left you alone and you considered moving out?" he persisted.

"You have to admit this is complicated."

"And uncomfortable and difficult?"

"Let's talk about something else," she said, unsure how she'd gotten herself into this.

"Are you bailing on me, Tate?"

"No." Too innocent.

"Are you so warm for my form that you're having trouble with our arrangement? Is that why it's uncomfortable and difficult?" he said with amusement and a satisfaction that somehow managed to be more charming than conceited.

Still, Josie sighed exaggeratedly and repeated, "Let's talk about something else."

"First I think you ought to let me know if you're bailing."

"I'm not bailing."

"But you *are* uncomfortable with the arrangement and it's difficult for you."

Josie rolled her eyes at him but refused to say anything at all.

He grinned as if that was answer enough.

Josie decided to try changing the subject.

"So I'm assuming that if you played poker it was a slow night."

"It was," he said. "But a slow night for me is a good thing for everyone else. It means no one's house or business burned down, nobody got hurt, there were no untoward events that required our services. Which was also lucky because I wouldn't have wanted to be needed for anything too serious with my mind wandering the way it was," he finished, neatly returning to what had gotten her into trouble initially.

But Josie wasn't taking the bait this time.

"This must be the deli you were talking about," she said instead, seizing the opportunity when she spotted the sign just ahead that announced Pomeranski's Delicatessen.

"That's it," he confirmed.

He went on to point out the bakery next to it and the bar across the street that he said served the best onion rings in the world.

In the middle of his description about what exactly made them the best onion rings in the world, an elderly couple came around the corner. Since Michael knew them, they paused to talk and to be introduced to Josie.

The four of them chatted a few minutes before Michael said he had to get Josie home.

As they left the older couple, he leaned very close and said into her ear, "They're my mother's neighbors—that's why I had to do the whole fiancée bit."

"I figured they probably knew her somehow," Josie said, once more fighting those flutters in her stomach at the intimacy of having his breath brush her skin.

"So how did you decide to be a fireman?" she asked then, hoping that since some time had elapsed they might be able to have a simple conversation minus all the innuendoes.

He didn't answer readily and she had the impression he was debating about whether or not to finally let her off the hook. But apparently he decided to because he said, "My dad was a volunteer firefighter and I think the first time I saw him in the gear I knew that was what I wanted to do, too."

"He was only a volunteer? I mean, not to diminish it, but he also did something else?"

"He was a midlevel businessman. He worked the administration end of an insurance company," Michael said without seeming to have taken offense to her "only a volunteer" comment. "But my dad was very big on giving something back to the community. He was committed to it. And being a fireman nights and weekends was the way he chose to do it. I was proud of him for that."

"How old were you when you lost him?" Josie asked, knowing only that his father had passed away, not how or when.

"I was twelve. He died fighting an office building fire."

That surprised her. "He did?"

Michael glanced at her. "How did you think he died?"

"I hadn't really thought about it. But I guess I

must have figured he'd had a heart attack or been killed in a car accident or something.''

''No, he was in the building when the floor collapsed. He fell through and was killed instantly.''

''I'm sorry,'' Josie said, much as Michael had to her when she'd told him about her parents' deaths.

''Me, too,'' Michael answered the same way she had. ''But at least I still had my mother and my sister,'' he added, referring to the fact that she'd been orphaned.

''And you went on wanting to be a firefighter yourself even after losing your dad like that?'' she asked in amazement.

''Yeah, my mom thought I was crazy, too. But I guess it was just in my blood. I did a lot of other things to put myself through college. I joined the National Guard. But when it was time to choose what I was going to do, my heart was still in the fire fighting.''

''You wanted to be like the dad you were proud of,'' Josie surmised.

''When I was a kid, sure. But that wasn't the driving force when I made my choice of occupations. What really stuck was the serving-the-community thing. I believe in that, too. Even if it might sound hokey to some people.''

''I don't think it sounds hokey,'' Josie said, meaning it and thinking that she'd just learned yet another thing about him that impressed her.

But finding more things that impressed her about him was counterproductive to the goal she'd set for herself so she altered the subject slightly. "It must have been hard on your mother and sister to lose your father so early, too. Did your mom have to go out and support the family then?"

"There was insurance money and benefits from the state, so she managed without working outside the home. But yes, it was tough. To tell you the truth, I always wished she *would* get a full-time job. Then maybe she would have met some people, had more of a life. As it was, her total focus was on me."

"What about Cindy?"

"It's always been the way it was when we were there for dinner the other night. In case you didn't notice, my mother treats my sister as if Cindy is part of the wallpaper. I'm the golden child and Cindy…well, Cindy is incidental."

"I noticed but I thought maybe it just had to do with the occasion—you know, you'd brought your new fiancée home and that put the attention on you and me."

"No, the way it was Monday night is just the way it is."

"It sounded like your mother is trying to fix your sister up about as much as she's been trying to fix you up, though."

"Oh, yeah, she's doing that, all right. But on the whole you'll find that my mother's attitude toward Cindy is different. And for me, once my father was gone, being the focal point of her life wasn't a breeze."

"Doesn't your mother like your sister?"

"Oh, sure. But my mother was raised in a family of six kids—all the rest of them boys. She was treated like the maid. She had to work alongside her mother, cooking and cleaning and doing the laundry—that was what women did. But her brothers... They really were the family jewels."

Michael tossed her a devilish smile to let her know he enjoyed the return to what he'd teased her about before.

"Behave," Josie warned.

He did but he was clearly still enjoying himself.

"Anyway," he continued, "I always thought that after being treated like that herself, my mother would have been determined *not* to do it to her daughter. But instead she does the same thing— I'm the major award and Cindy is the consolation prize."

"I feel bad for her. What does she think about it?"

"Sometimes it gets to her and sometimes she has a sense of humor about it. But for the most part she says she recognizes that it isn't her, personally, who Mom considers less valuable, it's *all* women. Cindy knows Mom loves her. It's just the way Mom was brought up—believing the males in the family are the important members—and there's nothing we can do about it."

"But you try," Josie said. "You try to get your mother to see that Cindy has worth, too, to even things out. You just aren't very successful at it."

"How do you know I do that?" he asked.

"I saw some of it at dinner. You kept turning

the spotlight on Cindy, praising her, pointing out the positives about her. Until now I thought it was only because you and your sister were close. That it was nice.'' And yet another thing she'd liked about him even before she'd known there was method to his madness.

But again thinking about his attributes did not aid her cause so she did her best to push it to the back of her mind.

''I'd just like it if Mom would give Cindy a little recognition,'' Michael said. ''And me a little breathing room.''

''I thought that was what I was for,'' Josie said with a laugh.

''I said breathing room, not *heavy* breathing.''

He was teasing her again. At least, she thought he was.

They'd made a big loop through the neighborhood and arrived back at the brownstone, naturally putting an end to the banter so Josie didn't feel the need to berate him again.

They climbed the steps and Michael used his key, holding the door open for Josie to go in first.

Pip had apparently heard them coming because he was waiting to pounce the moment they stepped across the threshold.

Pip was an equal-opportunity greeter. The bull mastiff jumped up exuberantly on them both, going back and forth to lick ears and cheeks and to whine like a baby.

Unlike a lot of other people Josie knew, Michael didn't balk at the reception. He patted Pip affectionately and gave the big dog a hearty rub before he threw Pip's stuffed beaver toy so the dog would chase it and let them get more than a foot into the living room.

Josie flipped on the light and then happened to catch a glimpse of Michael. And the havoc Pip had wreaked on the collar of his shirt.

"Here, let me fix the damage my dog did," she said, going to Michael to fold down his collar.

"Hold on a minute," he countered. "You're about to lose an earring."

"Pip?" she inquired.

"I think so," Michael answered, reaching for the U-shaped hook and the three bright beads that dangled from her lobe.

They were standing very close together. Facing each other. Once he'd adjusted her earring he didn't take his hand away. Instead he laid it against the side of her neck as their eyes seemed to lock with a will of their own. The heat of his touch ran through Josie like hot lava.

Okay, enough! she told herself. Move away!

But her body didn't respond to the command and she stayed right where she was, staring up into those vibrant green eyes as they searched her own.

And then dropped slowly to her mouth.

He's going to kiss me….

He's going to kiss me….

Please, kiss me….

Then he did.

It was a light kiss. A chaste kiss. Nothing like the mad, passionate kisses of Labor Day weekend.

Yet somehow that simple, sweet meeting of their lips had a special quality all its own.

A special quality that made her so sorry when he ended it long before she was ready for him to.

But after only a few moments, he pulled his hand from its warm caress of her skin. Even though he didn't step back, he sort of straightened away from her, putting inches between them that felt to Josie like miles.

He smiled, though. A naughty-boy smile.

"We've never done that, have we?" he said in a deep voice.

Did he have amnesia? They'd kissed more times than she could count. "We've never done what?" she asked, confused.

"Anything with inhibition."

That made her smile because it was so true. "No, I guess we haven't."

"But I probably wasn't supposed to do it one way or another, was I?"

"Well, it was more than a friendly handshake," she pointed out.

"And more than the kind of kiss I'd give my mother or my sister," he contributed.

"So, no, it probably shouldn't have been done," Josie agreed. But only halfheartedly.

They continued to stand there, face-to-face and near enough that Josie could still feel the heat of him and the charged energy that was in the air between them.

She knew she should be distancing herself from

him. That she should be chastising herself—and maybe him, too—mercilessly.

But the best she could do was say, "We should probably call it a night."

Michael nodded. "Probably should." Then, parodying what they'd both just said so many times, he said, "Probably should. Probably shouldn't. Probably, probably, probably..."

But neither of them moved. Or broke the lock that held them gazing into each other's eyes.

"You have another twenty-four-hour shift tomorrow, right?" she asked, her voice breathier than she wished it was.

"I do."

"So I guess I'll see you Friday then."

"You will."

Still neither of them budged.

But only for another moment before Josie reminded herself that this was not the way things should be. Not the way they could be.

She finally spun on her heels, fleeing from the force field that seemed to have held her there.

"I'll just let Pip out and then get to bed," she announced as if nothing at all had happened.

"Go ahead on up. I think I can use a little more air so I'll take Pip in back and throw the ball for him for a while."

She wanted to ask why Michael needed air but she didn't. She just said, "Okay. He'll come find his bed when you're finished. Thanks."

"For?"

"Playing with Pip."

Michael raised his chin in acknowledgment, apparently having thought she was thanking him for something else. The kiss, maybe?

"See you Friday, then," Josie said as she headed for the stairs.

But before she even reached them, Michael's voice stopped her. "You know, even though I gave you a hard time about it tonight, I'm having some trouble with this myself," he said as if admitting something against his will.

Josie angled a questioning glance at him.

"The stuff about this being complicated and difficult. And uncomfortable," he clarified. "Although I think *dis*comfort is probably a better term."

"*Dis*comfort? I'm causing you pain?"

He grinned a grin that was wicked and sexy and insinuative all at once. "A world of hurt," he confirmed, letting her know he was talking about the sexual tension between them. And the inability to have it satisfied.

"So, would you rather I move out?" she asked.

He shook his handsome head. "I'm not bailing on you, either."

"You also aren't behaving yourself," Josie pointed out as if she hadn't done her own bit of stepping over the line.

"I'll do better from here on," he promised.

"Good," she answered.

Then she went up the stairs.

But she went feeling like a hypocrite.

Because Michael's promise that he would do

better from here on was not what she wanted deep down.

What she wanted deep down was the promise of something entirely different.

The promise his lips on hers had given...

Chapter Five

"I said you'd have to wait and that's what you'll have to do. I'll let you know when Eloise is available."

"Are we a little PMSy today?"

Josie had gone to get her purse. When she returned to her desk at eleven-thirty Friday morning, she came in on the heated exchange between Allison Baker and a reporter.

The reporter had shown up unexpectedly an hour before, asking if Eloise Vale would see her for an impromptu interview about how the mayor's proposed budget cuts would affect Manhattan Multiples. Eloise had agreed, but since she already had another meeting scheduled the reporter would have to wait until Eloise was free.

"I'm sure it'll just be a few more minutes. When I went by Eloise's office just now she was saying goodbye to the person she was in a meeting with," Josie informed the reporter who was not someone they wanted to alienate.

"That's all I was asking—how much longer," the reporter said huffily. Then she left the front of the kiosk to return to one of the chairs in the waiting room.

When she did, Josie turned to Allison. "Are you sure you don't mind my leaving early for lunch and sticking you with receptionist duties on top of your other work? I know you're busy. If you have too much going on I can cancel and wait for another day when Leah is here," Josie offered, concerned that the favor she'd asked of Allison was the cause for Allison's short temper today.

"It's only half an hour," Allison snapped. "It's no big deal.

Maybe Allison *was* a little PMSy. Although Josie had worked with her for several months and never found that to be the case before. Allison was ordinarily very even-tempered.

"Are you okay?" Josie ventured.

"I just have some things on my mind," Allison said, obviously forcing control.

"This lunch was a last-minute thing. Really, I could beg off without any problem. Maybe you and I could order something in after everyone else leaves and have lunch together instead. If you wanted to talk," Josie offered.

Allison seemed to deflate slightly and when she

shook her head she looked so upset and forlorn Josie's heart went out to her.

But Allison only said, "No. Thanks. I guess maybe I am kind of cranky today, but it's nothing I can talk about. Just go and I promise I'll try not to bite off anybody else's head while you're gone."

Still, Josie was concerned about her and wanted to help in any way she could, so she said, "How about if I bring you back something to eat?"

"I brought my lunch. Seriously, it's all right. Go ahead and enjoy yourself, and don't give me another thought."

"You're sure?" Josie asked.

"Positive."

"Okay," Josie conceded. "But I'm going down the street to your favorite little place—how about if I bring you back a slice of Chocolate Indulgence at least?"

Allison laughed, whether at Josie's persistence or the thought that a chunk of chocolate could fix her problems. But either way, she said, "Okay."

Josie gave her co-worker's shoulder a squeeze and said, "Great. Just hang on until I get back and you'll have the chocolate cure-all."

"I'll try," Allison joked.

Josie left the office then, hoping this lunch wasn't a mistake all the way around. Not only was she leaving Allison to cover for her when Allison was apparently in a bad mood, but the lunch was with Elsa Dunnigan—Michael's mother.

Elsa had called her earlier that morning to say

she was going to be in Manhattan today and would Josie meet her for lunch. The older woman hadn't given her any reason for it and Josie hoped it was merely a friendly gesture. But she didn't know Michael's mother well enough to be sure.

She also wondered if there was anything she should know before she had a meal alone with Elsa. But again this morning Michael had come home from his shift at the fire station and gone to bed before Josie had so much as said good morning to him. She hadn't wanted to wake him with a phone call to ask if it was okay that she have lunch with his mother.

So she was just going to wing it and hope that Elsa Dunnigan merely wanted to get to know her.

And that Allison didn't go ballistic before she got back.

The restaurant was a small lunch-counter-type place a short distance from the office. When Josie arrived, Elsa Dunnigan was already there at one of the tables that formed a semicircle around the counter.

The older woman spotted her as she came through the door and waved an arm high in the air to get her attention.

"Hi," Josie greeted her. "I'm sorry I'm a few minutes late. You know how it is trying to get out of a busy office. I hope you haven't been waiting long."

"I'm just glad you could come at all," Elsa said, taking a sip of a cup of coffee that was nearly empty.

Josie sat across from Michael's mother, who had the menu open in front of her. Since Josie was familiar with what was available, when their waitress came to ask if they were ready to order, they did.

After she left Josie said, "So what did you come into Manhattan for today? Shopping? An appointment?"

Elsa smiled sheepishly. "I made that up—about having to come into Manhattan. I really only wanted to see you."

"You didn't have to make anything up. You could have just called and said you wanted to have lunch."

"Would you have agreed?"

"Sure. Unless I couldn't for some reason. It's nice that you wanted to have lunch with me."

"Then next time I'll tell you the truth," Elsa said, looking pleased.

They'd both ordered sandwiches and the waitress brought them then, complete with potato salad, pickle spears, the soda Josie had ordered and a coffee refill for Elsa.

As soon as the waitress left them again, Michael's mother said, "I thought we could talk about the wedding."

Josie hadn't seen that one coming. She'd thought Elsa had understood any wedding was too far in the future to discuss yet. So that's what she said. "It's too soon to talk about that."

"Oh, it's never too soon. Even if it's a year away."

Josie remembered Michael specifically telling his mother it was more than a year away. Much more. But clearly Elsa had chosen to ignore him.

So Josie repeated that, too. "We're a lot more than a year away. So much more that it's too early to even think about it, let alone talk about it."

Elsa Dunnigan waved away that notion with her free hand as she fed herself a bite of potato salad with a fork in the other.

Then she said, "I know that's what Michael said. But that's just men. They need a little nudging in the matrimonial department. If you and I set a date and you tell him that's what you want, he'll agree. Mark my words. I saw how he looks at you. You can get him to do whatever you want."

That was Josie's second shock. "I think you're imagining things," she blurted before she considered if that might offend her lunch companion.

Elsa didn't seem offended, though. She just laughed. "I'm not imagining anything. I know my son and, believe me, I've seen him around enough women to know the difference between the way he looks at you and the way he's looked at everyone else. He'd jump off a cliff for you."

Apparently, Michael was a better actor than Josie had guessed. Although she couldn't help wondering what it was his mother had thought she'd seen.

Still, Josie decided she'd better try a different tack with the older woman.

"I'm the one who wants a long engagement," Josie insisted, putting strong emphasis on the *I* part of that. "Michael and I have really just met and even though we were impulsive enough to get engaged and move in together, we really do need to get to know each other before we even start to talk about a wedding."

"Not just a wedding. *Your* wedding," Elsa corrected. "And it will take a long time to plan it. You and I and Cindy will have to shop for your dress. We'll all have to go to cake tastings and catering samplings. We'll need hours to pour through bridal magazines for ideas for flower arrangements and decorations. There's the ceremony itself—I don't know what you think about it, but I always like it when the vows are said under an arch. A white, lattice arch, maybe. With flowers and vines—"

"Wait, wait, wait," Josie said with a laugh.

It all sounded like fun and if she and Michael really were engaged it would have been really nice to have this woman so eager to accept her into the fold, to shop with her and to participate in all the planning the way she would have wanted her own mother to. But she and Michael weren't really engaged, and she just couldn't let his mother go on.

"Please, Elsa, you're getting way ahead of us. Honestly, Michael and I are nowhere near ready to set a date, let alone shop for a dress or taste cakes. I don't even know what kind of cake he likes yet."

"Chocolate," Elsa said as if that solved everything.

"Okay. But still, he and I need to get to know each other much, much better before we go any further than we already have. And you and I need to get to know each other, too. Let's just work on that for now.''

''I already know I like you. The rest can come over the years.''

''See? Over the years—we have lots of time. There's no rush.''

Elsa had finished half her sandwich and she pushed her plate away, meticulously pulling only her refilled coffee cup toward her.

During the brief silence that accompanied the switch, Josie hoped she'd successfully stemmed the flow of wedding plans. But when the other woman spoke again it seemed more that Elsa was just trying another tack.

''You know, I wasn't too sure Michael was ever going to actually give in and find a wife. I've been trying to get him to for a long while now. But he's been so resistant. I don't know why, but he's avoided any serious involvement like the plague. I've always thought that he saw how happy his father and I were together, and that that should have made him want the same thing. But for some reason it didn't.''

''Michael told me about his dad's death,'' Josie said for lack of anything else to say.

''That alone is a sign of how close he feels to you already. He never talks about his dad,'' Elsa said pointedly. Then she seemed to open up to Josie. ''It was hard on us all. The kids lost their father. I lost a man who was more than my husband. He was my best friend. My soul mate…''

"How long were you married?"

"Fifteen years. But we were together more than five years before that. We started dating in the seventh grade and we were never apart from then on."

"That's amazing."

"It is. It was," Elsa agreed.

She had a far-off look in her eyes for a moment before she refocused on Josie. "I can see the same thing between you and Michael that was between his father and me."

"Oh, I don't know about that," Josie demurred, feeling even more guilty for the lies she and Michael were telling. It just seemed awful to have his mother believe that she was seeing her own true love reflected in the sham they were perpetrating.

"No, I can see that you and Michael have what his father and I had," Elsa insisted. "There's something about the two of you. You go together. Besides, I've always been convinced that his father's death has left a scar that's kept Michael from committing to a woman. Until now. So to have gotten past that, what he's found in you has to run even deeper than the scar."

Josie really felt bad. But what could she do? She couldn't vigorously refute what the other woman was saying without giving away the lies.

So instead she opted for a different course.

"Tell me about Michael's dad," she urged, hoping that was close enough to the subject not to seem like a change but that it would send Elsa in a different direction just the same.

"My Mike was one of a kind. A wonderful

man,'' Elsa said with an almost dreamy quality to her voice.

She went on to describe her late husband in detail and Josie was granted her wish—Elsa got lost in her memories and finally stopped comparing her relationship with Michael's father to Josie's relationship with Michael.

But the things Michael's mother said about Michael's father were so sweet, so endearing, so private, that Josie was torn between feeling ashamed of herself for being allowed the confidence under false pretenses, and honored to hear it.

And then their lunch was over and Josie needed to get back to work.

Elsa insisted on paying the bill, putting in another plug for at least setting a wedding date and beginning the planning as they left the restaurant. Only this time Josie had the excuse of work to escape the other woman's dogged persistence.

But as Josie retraced her steps she couldn't help thinking about Michael's mother. About the torch the older woman still carried for the man she'd lost eighteen years ago.

And while on the one hand Josie wondered if she would ever know that kind of love herself, on the other hand her belief that it was better not to allow herself a love like that and risk suffering the pain of losing it, was reinforced.

''I didn't know if you'd be here or not,'' Josie said to Michael as she came into the brownstone that evening after work.

She'd seen him looking out the picture window in the living room when she'd walked up the steps. He'd spotted her and left the window to open the door for her.

"Where did you think I'd be?" he asked as she came inside.

"On a date, maybe?" Josie answered, setting her purse down but keeping hold of the videotape she'd rented and the brown bag that held the take-out food she'd planned to have for dinner.

"Nope, no date," Michael said.

Which would explain the fact that he was dressed in a pair of time-aged jeans and a plain white T-shirt—not going-out attire, even though he looked terrific with his shoulders and every honed muscle of his torso cupped by that shirt, and his lower half hugged by denim that seemed to have memorized his perfect form.

"I was just watching for you," he said, "hoping you wouldn't be tied up, either."

"Oh?" That sounded so simple and uncomplicated. Unlike what Josie was feeling at just the idea that he might have wanted to spend the evening with her.

"I have to pull a double shift over the weekend," he said. "That means I leave here tomorrow morning and don't come home until Monday morning."

Learning that deflated Josie's spirits, but it didn't explain why he'd been hoping she wouldn't be tied up tonight.

"If you're worried that I'll bring in a bunch of

people and keep you awake too late tonight, you can relax,'' she said, still fishing for a clue to his motives.

''I wasn't worried about that, no. I just wanted to see you before I have to be gone for that long,'' he said simply.

They were on thin ice when either of them so openly admitted something like that. But it thrilled Josie just the same.

''So, do you have a date?'' he asked.

''No. It's been a long week. I just thought I'd relax, eat Chinese food and watch a movie.'' She held up the sack. ''I have plenty, if you're hungry.''

Actually she'd purposely ordered more than she could ever eat, telling herself it was only common courtesy to bring home enough for Michael, too, just in case. But the truth was, when she'd ordered extra she'd been hoping they might end up sharing the food. Despite knowing she'd be better off if they didn't.

''What'd you get?'' he asked, eyeballing the bag.

''Lettuce wraps. Crab wontons. Mongolian beef. And crispy, honey-orange-peel shrimp.''

''And the movie?''

She handed him the video so he could see for himself. It wasn't a recent film. It was an older romantic comedy about two people whose paths cross at several different stages in life until they finally become friends and then fall in love.

''Chinese food and a chick flick,'' Michael summarized after reading the blurb on the box. But he said it with a smile that brightened his handsome, freshly shaved face. "I've never seen this, though. So I'm up for it. If you don't mind the company."

"Company's always good." Except when the guy providing the company made her pulse quicken and the entire prospect of the evening ahead of her seem like a hundred times more fun than it had originally. Or when the guy providing the company was the same guy she could never seem to get out of her head despite her every attempt. Having company like that was more in the "living dangerously" category.

But she didn't say that.

"Do you want to change out of your work clothes before we eat?" Michael asked.

"Friday night flake-out—that means I change my clothes, we start the movie and eat out of the cartons in front of the television."

Again Michael smiled. "My kind of woman."

The whole time Josie was changing into her jeans and a tie-dyed, crew-neck T-shirt—a T-shirt that did some body-hugging of its own—she lectured herself about keeping this evening in perspective. Michael merely hadn't wanted to go out on the town because he was about to do a forty-eight-hour shift. And since he was going to be home, anyway, he'd probably just wanted someone to hang out with. Anyone would likely have filled the bill. Any friend. Any roommate. She just happened to be the roommate. The plain, old, everyday roommate who just happened to bring home an overabundance of food so she didn't have to be rude and eat in front of him.

She swore to herself that there was no more to it on either side.

Then she put a comb through her hair, powdered her nose and refreshed her lip gloss.

And tried to tamp down on the excitement that was flooding through her at the prospect of spending tonight alone with Michael....

The movie was one of Josie's favorites. She'd seen it a half dozen times before. But watching it with someone who had never seen it made it all the more enjoyable for her.

Or maybe just sitting on the sofa next to Michael accomplished that.

Either way, by the time the food was gone and the film had ended, she was anything but ready to call it a night. So as they clicked off the TV and the VCR, Josie angled toward Michael on the couch, pulled one of her legs up underneath her and said, "I had lunch with your mother today."

"Oh, that can't be good," Michael said gravely.

Josie laughed at him. "It wasn't bad."

He didn't look convinced. "How did that come about?" he asked.

"She called me at work first thing this morning and said she'd be in Manhattan and would I have lunch with her."

"She'd be in Manhattan?" he repeated suspiciously. "For what?"

"I know—she made it sound like there was a

reason other than having lunch with me. But then she confessed that there wasn't.''

"Let me guess—she wanted to have lunch with you to push you into setting a wedding date.''

"And into starting to make plans.''

Michael rolled his eyes. "The woman is unbelievable.''

"It was okay. I got around it. I just held the line about us wanting time to get to know each other and not being anywhere near ready to set a date, let alone make plans.''

"Did she accept that?'' he asked as if he knew the answer.

"No. I just caved and we're getting married a week from tomorrow,'' Josie said with a straight face.

Still, Michael got the joke and couldn't help smiling.

"She had to accept it because I didn't give her any choice,'' Josie said emphatically.

"Well, just be warned, this is only the first attack. Knowing my mother she'll be a broken record about this. You're probably going to end up asking me for hazard pay.''

"It's okay. I really like your mom.''

That seemed to surprise him. "You do?''

"I do. Sure, she's kind of overbearing, but she's not mean-spirited or anything. And it made me feel good to have a mom—even someone else's mom—doing the mother-of-the-bride thing with me. Even if I'm not really going to be a bride. Remember, I haven't had a mother of my own since I was a little kid and here is your mom, taking me under her wing, acting like I'm one of the family. I thought it was nice.''

"I never said she wasn't nice," Michael pointed out. "Just pushy."

Josie laughed again. "She's that. But only because she wants what she thinks is best for you. Because she loves you. She's not hurtful or anything. It think that's sweet."

Michael smiled. "I'm glad you see it all that way. I know a lot of people who wouldn't. And who wouldn't appreciate my mother's tactics."

"So you don't mind if I share her a little?"

Now he looked all-out shocked. "No, I don't mind. I think that's great. In fact, I appreciate it. I love her and she's important to me. She can just be a pain in the neck," he said, ending with a laugh himself. "Your liking her and not dreading having to see her makes this whole situation easier all the way around."

"She had some things to say about you, too," Josie told him then, using it to fish a second time tonight. This time for information to satisfy the curiosity his mother's comments had left her with.

Michael repositioned himself slightly, facing her more and resting a long arm on the top of one of the sofa's back cushions. "What did she say?"

Josie opted not to tell him his mother had said anything about the way he looked at her or that there were similarities she thought she saw between their relationship and the relationship his parents had had. But she did say, "Your mom doesn't understand how you could have seen her and your dad together and not have ended up wanting the same thing for yourself. Why you've avoided any serious involvement with a woman.'' Josie paused a moment. ''Have you avoided any serious involvement with any woman?''

''Pretty much,'' he admitted. ''I've only been in short-term relationships.''

''So she was right. Has it always been on purpose?''

''As a matter of fact, it has. If it looks like I'm getting in too deep—or the woman is—I put an end to it.''

When they'd agreed after their weekend together that they didn't want any kind of serious involvement, Josie had taken it at face value. She hadn't thought it had any deep-rooted basis on Michael's part. Now she did.

''You always end a relationship if either of you start to have any kinds of feelings that might develop into more than a passing fancy?'' she said to make sure.

''Always.''

''Why do you do that?'' she asked without any criticism, simply out of curiosity.

Michael didn't rush to answer that and in the silence Josie thought that he might keep her in the dark the same way he'd apparently kept his mother in the dark. Especially since even when he broke the silence he wasn't forthcoming.

He said, ''My folks did have an amazing relationship. They were wild for each other. And supportive. A team in the best sense of the word. Passionately in love. So hot for each other that, as a kid, it was embarrassing. But it really was something.''

''Just not something you wanted for yourself?'' Josie persisted.

''It's definitely something I wanted for myself. Something I still want for myself.''

''But only with a woman of your choosing, not with a woman your mother chooses for you?'' Josie guessed, trying to make sense of what, so far, didn't seem to.

''It doesn't matter who chooses the woman as long as she's the *right* woman. At the right time.''

Somehow that seemed like a clue. ''Why does 'at the right time' sound like it carries as much weight as the 'right woman' part of that?'' she asked, being nosy because she wanted to know what made him tick and she had a feeling that whatever was going on in his head about relationships was a big portion of it.

Such a big portion of it that once again Michael didn't answer readily. In fact, he stared off into the distance and let an even longer silence pass before he finally seemed to decided to answer her. ''I'm not going to get married or have kids until I retire.''

For a moment Josie thought he was kidding. But then she realized his expression was too solemn for that to be the case.

''I've known people who want to wait. But isn't that waiting a little too long?'' she said, injecting some humor into her tone to lighten the weighty mood her questions seemed to have sunk him into.

"It's not as long as it sounds," he said. "I can retire after twenty-five years service—that will make me forty-seven. Granted that's a little late for getting married and starting a family, but for me it's that way or no way."

"Why?" Josie asked again, not beating around the bush.

"I lost my father in a fire, remember?" he said as if the answer should be obvious. "I told you I always knew I wanted to be a firefighter. But I couldn't resolve that with the possibility that something could happen to me the way it did to my dad. That I could leave a wife and kids to go through what my mother and Cindy and I did. So I came to the conclusion that if I was going to do this and take the risk, I had to do it solo."

"And your mother doesn't know that?" Josie asked, thinking that it was something Elsa should have been aware of.

"I tried to tell her once. But she blew it off. She said any amount of time she had—*we* had—with my dad was worth it. And she went right on fixing me up with every woman she knows anyway."

"She didn't take you seriously?" And he *was* serious about this. That was clear.

"She didn't want to hear it so she just let it go in one ear and out the other."

"But it really is a factor to you."

"A huge factor," he confirmed. "A huge factor that was reinforced with the destruction of the

World Trade Center. I saw too many wives and kids of police and firefighters left behind. Left to suffer that same agony my family had suffered. Left to struggle with it all. And even if I had moments ·when I doubted my decision before, I haven't since then. It was such a glaring example of just what I'd thought—that I couldn't have a wife and kids and still do this job. That I didn't feel right taking the risk for anyone but myself. That it wouldn't be fair to take it for anyone but myself."

"Did you tell your mom that then? After 9/11?"

"No. Why bother? She wouldn't have listened to that any more than she'd listened to me before. She can't get it out of her head that I need to get married and have a family. Now. Because that's what she wants."

"I'm only postulating so don't take this as anything carved in stone, but when your mom was talking today I had the feeling that maybe she sees your not getting involved as you holding back from all of life because of your father's death. Maybe she can't believe you've completely gotten over it until you can commit to someone."

"If that's what she thinks, it's crazy," Michael said.

But he said it so quickly, so defensively, that Josie had to wonder if his mother wasn't right, after all.

"On the other hand, if it's true that that's where my mom's coming from," he added, "then I guess the upside of our fake engagement is that it will put her mind to rest. So it benefits me and her, too.''

''I suppose there is that,'' Josie agreed, even though she doubted that was anything more than a rationalization.

The conversation seemed to find an end then. Michael took a deep breath and stretched as if he'd been in one position for too long. He reached his arms high in the air and arched his back, expanding his remarkable chest until it stretched the limits of his T-shirt and nearly made Josie's eyes pop out of their sockets.

To make matters worse, he even writhed a little and the expression on his face reminded her of more intimate times when that same look of satisfaction had come over him. Times when they'd been lying with arms and legs entwined. With breaths mingling. With bodies glistening. Satiated. Spent. And feeling so good it was impossible to recall it and not want to be there again...

Josie was wrestling with that memory, trying to force it and her response to it back into the recesses of her mind when he finished his stretch and relaxed back into the cushions of the couch.

''I should probably turn in and get some sleep while I can. If it's a busy weekend I'll be lucky to catch catnaps,'' he said, oblivious to what he'd just set off in her.

''How come you're doing a double shift?'' she asked, working to sound normal when she felt anything but.

''Two of our guys are out. One had to have

emergency surgery and the other went to Detroit to get married. The rest of us are covering their hours while they're gone.''

''So you'll work the whole weekend?'' Dumb. He'd told her that.

But rather than realizing that Josie was preoccupied with taming desires she didn't want to be having, Michael misinterpreted her questioning him about something she already knew and said, ''Why? Will you miss me?''

''Miss you? When I have Pip?'' she said, finally managing to get a grip and respond in the same teasing vein.

''You're putting me in the dog's league?'' he asked in mock outrage.

''Hey, I love my dog,'' she said flippantly.

Michael's grin widened. ''Are you telling me you love me?''

''As roommates go, I'm just googly-eyed for you,'' she joked.

''Uh-huh,'' he murmured, letting her know he knew she didn't mean it.

Then he dropped the teasing and said, ''I enjoyed the movie. Every time they'd show one of those old couples sitting on the sofa telling the story of how they met I'd think about us.''

Josie laughed. *''When Michael Met Josie?''* she said, playing off the movie's title. Then, using a tone like the elderly couples who had done in-a-nutshell descriptions of the courses of their courtships, she said, ''When we met, we got carried away.''

"And then we agreed to never see each other again," Michael said, playing his part by telling the next stage.

"And then we *did* see each other again, and we decided to live together and *pretend* to be engaged," she supplied.

"But only as friends," he said.

"Only as friends," Josie confirmed.

But that fact notwithstanding, her voice had suddenly become soft and breathy. Because what had begun as a game had ended with her looking into those incredible green eyes of his as they probed hers.

"Just friends," he repeated, his tone more than merely friendly, too. Husky. Sexy. Insinuative.

Then, without warning, Michael reached a hand to the side of her face. More than a friendly hand. A caressing hand that smoothed her skin with a tender, seductive thumb as his eyelids lowered to half-mast and his gaze slowly slid to her mouth.

She knew what he was going to do and no amount of telling herself not to let him made any difference. How could it when she wanted to kiss him as badly as she wanted him to kiss her?

And when he did she couldn't help but melt. His warm, supple mouth met hers, lingering longer than he had the previous evening.

No, tonight there was no hurry. Tonight he kissed her and he went right on kissing her.

She could have pulled away. She knew she should have. But she didn't. And neither did he.

In fact, he did more than linger. His lips parted,

urging hers to part, too, and he deepened the kiss, turning it into the kind of kisses that had gotten her into his bed in the first place.

Stop this, she ordered herself.

But she didn't.

Instead her lips parted in response to that urging. And worse still, her hand rose to the side of his neck, snaking around to his nape where she could feel the short bristles of his hair. Where she could absorb the heat of his skin while mouths opened even wider and his tongue came to tease the inner edges of her lips, to meet tip to tip her tongue and coax it to play.

Not that much coaxing was required. In spite of knowing with every fiber of her being that she shouldn't let this go on, Josie just had to. She just had to go on kissing him back, welcoming his tongue with hers, matching him circle for circle, dance for dance, parry for thrust.

His hand deserted her face so he could wrap her in both big, strong arms and pull her closer. Close enough for her breasts to press against him as her nipples hardened, nudging into those honed pectorals as mouths opened even wider, as the kiss turned hungry and demanding.

But somewhere in the midst of it Josie's words of moments before about them getting carried away began to ring in her ears. Because she knew they were on the brink of that.

She also knew that while on so many levels Michael was everything any woman would want—

including her—on one very crucial level he was absolutely what she couldn't let herself have.

So she mustered up every ounce of willpower she owned, laid her palms against his massive chest, and pushed herself away, ending the kiss.

"Just friends," she reminded feebly, her voice barely a whisper and echoing with the desire she was unable to conceal.

But luckily Michael didn't argue. Or try to kiss her again.

All he did was smile a slow, mischievous smile and let her go.

"Can we call it just a little kissing between friends?" he joked then, his own voice ragged and rough with the effects of that kiss.

"I think we better call it a night," she said.

Michael nodded but he didn't jump to his feet. And neither did she. They stayed where they were, separated by mere inches, eyes still holding each other.

Until Josie made herself break the contact that was almost tangible.

"I'll let Pip out and lock up. You can get to bed," she said, fleeing the sofa as if it had suddenly burst into flames.

"Okay," Michael agreed, standing himself then.

"Come on, Pip, let's go outside," she called to the dog lounging near the coffee table as she headed for the kitchen.

Pip joined her at the swinging door but before Josie had the chance to go through it, Michael said, "Should I apologize for kissing you?"

With one hand on the panel Josie paused, not certain how to answer that.

But in the end she opted not to lie to him.

"No. It was as much me as you," she confessed. "We just have to not do that. We really have to be only friends."

"Right. Only friends. I completely agree. At least until I'm forty-seven and then maybe you should watch out. Big time," he added, joking about what he'd told her seriously earlier.

It managed to lighten the tone, though, and make Josie laugh. "Oh, don't worry, I know I have to watch out for you. Forty-seven or not."

Michael smiled at her so sweetly, she just wanted to forget everything and run back into his arms. But of course she didn't. She fought it as he said, "I guess I'll see you sometime Monday, then."

"I'll hold down the fort while you're gone."

He nodded but he still didn't say good-night. He just went on watching her with a look in his eyes that let her know he wanted her back in his arms as much as she wanted to be there.

But neither of them budged.

Until Pip barked—apparently tired of waiting to be let out.

"See you Monday," she said.

"Right. Have a nice weekend."

Josie merely nodded and finally managed to actually get through the door into the kitchen, leaving Michael behind.

But she doubted she'd have too nice a weekend no matter what.

Because knowing he wouldn't be around took all the luster right off it.

Chapter Six

The weekend felt strange to Josie. She was restless, which wasn't like her. She couldn't write no matter how hard she tried, which *really* wasn't like her. She couldn't focus. She couldn't get into watching television or the movie she rented. Even throwing the ball for Pip was a problem because by the time the big dog brought it back for her to throw again her mind was somewhere out in the ozone.

And there was only one thing to blame for it all.

Josie couldn't think about anything but Michael.

Damn him, anyway.

The way he looked, the things he said, the way he moved, his smile, his laugh—it was all there at the forefront of her brain no matter what she did to push it away.

She tried to tell herself she was merely bored. That she wasn't used to being alone for such a prolonged period of time. That on any other weekend before this she and Pip would have had the company of Sharon or one of their other roommates, or at least Sharon or their other roommates would have been coming and going and talking as they did to distract her.

But there she was, all alone, with nothing to dwell on but Michael.

Even trying not to think about him, even going over all the reasons why she shouldn't be thinking about him, ended with the same results—Michael was in her thoughts, in her mind's eye, in her every waking moment all weekend long.

So by Monday morning she was relieved to go back to work. To be out of that house. To be where she wouldn't have the scent of his aftershave lingering in the air. Where she wouldn't have reminders of him at every turn. Where she wouldn't be stuck reliving that kiss they'd shared on Friday night with every glance at the couch…

"Hi. I'm here for the breast-feeding multiples meeting."

Josie glanced up from sorting the day's mail to find a client on the other side of her kiosk. A petite, blond woman with freckles speckling her nose.

Josie assumed the woman was asking for directions and said, "Go right down that hall, the meeting is in the second room on the left. There's a sign on the door.''

"Oh, I know. I've already been there. It's just that I need to use the ladies' room and since I'm the first one here there's no one I can ask to keep an eye on the twins while I do. It might be silly of me but I can't get them in the stall and I just don't like them being outside of it all alone. Could I impose on you to watch them for just a few minutes?''

It wasn't such an unusual request and, as a rule, Josie would have asked Leah to do it. But Leah— the homeless mother-to-be Eloise had taken under her wing and employed at Manhattan Multiples doing light tasks here and there—had an appointment with her obstetrician and hadn't come in yet.

"No imposition,'' Josie assured the woman requesting assistance. ''I'd be happy to do it.''

The woman pushed the double stroller to Josie's side of the kiosk. ''Daniella and Darcy,'' she said, pointing out which was which before she dashed to the rest room.

"Hello, Daniella and Darcy,'' Josie said, turning her chair so she could face the stroller.

The two babies lying side by side looked to be not more than six weeks old. Josie didn't usually pay much attention to the babies brought into the office—she just wasn't interested in them. But for some reason these two seemed like the cutest little cherubs she'd ever seen.

They were identical, each with chubby cheeks,

turned-up noses, a smattering of curly red hair and green eyes. Green the color of Michael's eyes.

It was disheartening to find that she couldn't escape reminders of him even at work, but still, that's what she was thinking about as she let each baby take hold of an index finger.

The softest, chubbiest little hands curled around them reflexively and for no reason Josie could understand, it stirred something in her.

She started to feel the oddest twinges. Urges, almost.

She'd never felt them before. She'd never felt the slightest inclination to pick up one of the many babies brought into Manhattan Multiples. To hold one of them. To cuddle one of them. Certainly she hadn't ever looked at one of them and pictured them as her own.

But when she analyzed what was going through her, it occurred to her that that was just what she was doing.

It was so strange that Josie nearly laughed out loud. The very idea that she might be experiencing maternal feelings was so far out in left field it was funny.

Her? Free-spirited, lone-wolf Josie Tate even fleetingly thinking of herself in conjunction with *babies?*

Lord, maybe Michael's mother had been right and working at Manhattan Multiples was giving her baby fever.

Or did her attraction to Michael have something

to do with it? she wondered. After all, the thoughts, the inclinations, had cropped up at the same time she'd started thinking that the twins had his same color eyes.

That was a sobering possibility.

Until she told herself the whole thing was just too absurd to be true. That it was some kind of fluke. Some kind of weird flight of fancy. That it was nothing serious. Nothing real. Nothing to think twice about.

"You guys are just trying to confuse me," she whispered to the twins. "But it isn't going to work. No matter how cute you are."

Still, it flashed through her mind that Michael's babies might have those same beautiful eyes. That they might be just as cute. And that twinge started again.

"We're only roommates," she whispered defensively, as if the tiny infants had said otherwise.

One of the babies yawned and even that impressed Josie. Plus, their skin was so smooth she couldn't resist using the index finger Darcy released to gently rub one round cheek.

"You really are beautiful, though," she said, surprised by the awe in her own voice.

"Don't tell me you're taking notice of babies," Allison said as she came into the kiosk behind Josie.

Josie sat back in her chair in a hurry, as if she'd been caught doing something she shouldn't be.

"I'm just watching them while their mom is in the ladies' room."

"Come on, 'fess up. You were getting slobbery over them. I saw it. The armor of Miss Oblivious-To-The-Babies has finally cracked."

"Don't be silly," Josie said.

But her co-worker didn't seem convinced as she leaned over Josie's shoulder to look at the twins.

"They are adorable, aren't they?" Allison said then. "Look at that red hair."

"Mmm," Josie said noncommittally.

Daniella and Darcy's mother returned to retrieve her daughters. Allison told her how beautiful they were and after the other woman had thanked her, Allison picked up Eloise's stack of mail.

"Thanks for watching them," the twins' mother said to Josie.

"No problem," Josie said, glad they were being taken away before she suffered any more perplexing responses to them.

But she suffered one more anyway when the woman pushed the stroller out of the kiosk. Josie suddenly had a flash of more unfamiliar emotions.

She was sorry to see the twins go. And envious, too. And she couldn't help imagining herself with green-eyed babies.

With Michael's green-eyed babies...

"Uh-oh."

Uh-oh is right, she thought, alarmed by her own thoughts.

Then she realized Allison's "uh-oh" hadn't had

anything to do with that and she yanked herself out of her reverie to glance over her shoulder.

Allison had moved further down the desk and begun to open Eloise's mail. In her capacity as Eloise Vale's assistant it was part of her job to sort what was addressed to Eloise so she could present to their boss what needed immediate attention and what didn't.

"This is bad," Allison added.

Josie swiveled around on her chair to find that Allison's face had suddenly lost all color. "What's the matter?"

"This letter. It's a threat."

"Against Eloise?"

"Yes." Without taking her eyes off the sheet of notebook paper, Allison said, "It says she can't 'mess with a man's family and get away with it'— that's a quote."

"Who is the letter from?"

"It isn't signed. But it threatens to get even with her. To make her sorry she ever meddled in matters that don't concern her. To make everyone at Manhattan Multiples sorry."

"Should we call the police?"

Eloise joined them at the reception desk just in time to hear Josie's question.

"Call the police? Why would we call the police?" Eloise asked.

Allison showed her the letter and Josie watched as Eloise Vale's complexion paled, too.

"Well, this is just what we need around here on

top of everything else, isn't it?'' Eloise said when she'd finished reading it.

"Do you have any idea who it might be from?" Josie asked.

"No. But only a coward writes a letter like this and doesn't sign it."

"I don't think we should count on whoever sent that being too much of a coward to make good on the threats," Allison said. "You could be in real danger, Eloise."

"For what it's worth, I agree," Josie put in. "You shouldn't take something like that lightly."

Eloise was rereading the letter and, despite her attempts at bravado, it was clear by her expression that she was troubled.

"I suppose we should call the police to report it since there's reference made to all of Manhattan Multiples," she said after another moment. "I'm sure there's nothing they can do about it, but there should be record of it. Would you get them on the phone for me, Josie?"

"Right away," Josie assured her, picking up the receiver to do just that as Eloise left the kiosk with her head held high.

But even so, Josie knew the founder of Manhattan Multiples was shaken by that letter.

And suddenly her own unruly thoughts and the minor disruption of an attraction to Michael seemed much less important.

Josie's afternoon was hectic and stressful. Investigators for the police and for the postal service showed up to question the staff and clients who were on the premises. They also needed a list of current and past clients that Josie had to compile while still performing her usual duties.

The letter itself had been upsetting but the somber concerns of the investigators coupled with their suggestion that silent alarms with panic buttons be installed in both Eloise's office and at the reception desk increased the weightiness of the situation. By the end of the day Josie was only too glad to have it behind her.

Of course hoping Michael would be home when she got there didn't slow her steps any.

He was on the front stoop when she rounded the corner and Josie was thrilled to see him. Even if he was standing there with his mother.

Josie might have thought they were on their way out except that while Elsa Dunnigan was dressed in slacks and a light sweater, Michael's face was shadowed with a full day's growth of beard and he was wearing a ragged old football jersey and a pair of disreputable-looking blue jeans with holes in the knees.

His attire let Josie know that he was making good on the note he'd left on the message board in the kitchen Saturday morning. It had instructed her not to waste her weekend picking up around the house because Monday night would be house-cleaning night.

The note she'd avoided erasing until she'd gone

to bed the night before just to have the sight of his handwriting to look at over and over again...

"Hi," she greeted Michael and his mother.

"Hey," Michael said in response as Josie climbed the steps to the brownstone.

She went to stand at Michael's side the way she thought a fiancée would and smiled at Elsa.

"I'm so glad I get to see you before I go," Elsa said in return.

But rather than giving any reason for it she surveyed the two of them and when greetings were the only thing Michael and Josie exchanged, Elsa said to Michael, "Don't you kiss your fiancée when she comes home from work?"

"Not till you're gone," Michael answered, making it sound like saying hello would be too hot for the front stoop and his mother's eyes.

Josie chased away the ridiculous tingle that ran through her at just the thought of an intimate, private hello from him and turned her attention to Elsa. "You look nice. Are you headed out for the evening?"

"Dinner with a friend. I just thought I'd drop by on my way. Have you thought any more about letting me get started planning the wedding?"

Josie had no doubt that question was the reason Elsa was glad she got to see her.

But Michael answered before Josie could. "There's nothing to think about, Ma. You can't get started because it's too far off. So drop it, will you?"

"Maybe Josie doesn't want it to be that far off," Elsa countered.

"Yes, I do," Josie insisted. "We're in perfect agreement."

"See? You agree on things. Michael says you're spending tonight cleaning the house together—that means you're sharing the chores. You're already acting like a married couple. Why not make it legitimate?"

"It isn't *il*legitimate," Michael informed her with a laugh. "Now could you just go have your dinner and forget about it?"

"Marge will ask me when you're getting married and what will I tell her? That I don't know?" Elsa said, trying the same tack she'd used before.

"Yes," Michael answered simply enough.

"You're getting along, aren't you?" his mother asked, making it sound as if they needed to prove things were working out by setting a date.

"We're getting along great," Michael said enthusiastically. Then, to Josie, "Aren't we?"

"Great," Josie confirmed.

"I don't know. You aren't going near each other." Elsa's tone was goading.

"Oh, for crying out loud," Michael said, draping an arm across Josie's shoulders to pull her close to his side. "Are you happy now?"

Josie was. Although she knew it wasn't an emotion she should be feeling and had to remind herself that this was only for show.

"I'll be happy when you set a date," Elsa said, intractable as ever.

"Go have dinner," Michael commanded then with a voice full of frustration. "You already said you were going to be late."

Elsa glanced at her watch and apparently had to concede because she turned to go down the steps. "I also think we should consider an engagement ring," she said as she did.

"Who's 'we'? Are you carrying someone around in your pocket?" he said to her back.

"I'm just saying," Elsa said airily.

"Thanks for the advice," Michael responded facetiously.

But his tone didn't seem to bother his mother who called from the sidewalk, "Have a nice night."

"You, too." This from Michael.

"'Bye, Josie."

"'Bye, Elsa," Josie called with amusement in her voice.

Michael didn't move from his spot on the landing or from keeping his arm around Josie as they watched his mother leave.

And even though Josie knew it was altogether unwise, she couldn't help savoring that contact. Savoring the warmth and strength of his big body. The feel of his strong hand cupping her shoulder. Savoring the way she fit so snugly under his arm...

But the moment Elsa disappeared down the

street he broke the contact and turned back toward the house.

Josie was slightly slow in following him as she regrouped and once more pointed out to herself that there had been no substance to that physical contact. That it had been solely for the sake of appearances.

But still her body was difficult to convince.

When she finally had all the feelings his touch had inspired back under submission, she realized Michael was holding the door open, waiting for her.

She moved a lot faster then, going inside ahead of him without letting on that she was lamenting the loss of his arm across her shoulders or that she was mentally beating herself up for having liked it as much as she had.

Michael followed her into the house, closing the door behind them.

Then he said, ''Sorry you had to come home to that. I was trying to get her to leave before you got here but I didn't have much luck.''

''You can stop apologizing for your mother. She doesn't bother me,'' Josie assured.

He smiled a smile that made her knees go weak and she had to wonder how anyone dressed the way he was, with grungy whiskers darkening the lower half of his face, could still look so good to her.

But he did and she had to try to ignore it.

Although something about the expression on her

own face must have clued him into the fact that
she was thinking about his appearance because he
rubbed one hand over his beard and said, "I just
woke up about half an hour ago. I don't think I
had four hours sleep the whole weekend so I had
some catching up to do. I'll shower and shave after
we're done around here. That is, if you're up for
housecleaning. If you had a hard day and you don't
want to do this tonight—"

"I did have a hard day. Does it show?" she
asked with a laugh.

"No, you look great."

He said that as if he genuinely meant it, and it
went to her head a little more than it should have.

Then he said, "So do you want to skip the cleaning? Because believe me, it doesn't take much
arm-twisting to get me to forget it."

"No, that's okay. The place needs it and cleaning relaxes me." Besides the fact that doing anything with him was hardly a chore. "Just let me
change clothes and we can get started."

"I brought a bottle of wine home for later—I
thought when we finished we could reward ourselves with pizza and wine," he told her as she
headed for the stairs.

"That sounds good, too," she said with her foot
on the first step. "I'll be right back."

Josie changed into some ragged clothes of her
own. A pair of frayed jean shorts and a former
turtleneck T-shirt she'd cut the turtleneck out of
and the sleeves off of just above the elbows.

She also put a comb through her hair before she went back downstairs with a lilt to her step as if the simple change of outfit had wiped away all the effects of the day and left her rejuvenated. When it was actually the prospect of being with Michael that had done that.

"Okay, I'm all yours," she said when she found him in the kitchen getting cleaning supplies.

His grin was crooked and his tone was insinuative. "Really…"

"For cleaning," she qualified, secretly thrilled by the way his glance slid to her bare legs and lingered a moment before rising again.

"Divvy up the chores and let's get this place clean," she commanded.

He did that, taking the heavier work for himself and giving her the lighter, deciding that they could each take care of their own bed- and bathrooms, which Josie agreed with.

They went to work.

As the evening progressed they weren't side by side the whole time but their paths did cross. And whenever it did Josie couldn't help watching him surreptitiously.

Somehow when Michael did it, even vacuuming was something to see. Especially when she had the rear view of his to-die-for derriere in those jeans that not only fit him like an old friend, but also had a third hole in the back of one leg that gave her a peek of his thigh.

By the time the house was spotless it was after

nine and Josie needed a shower for more than to wash off housecleaning grime. She needed it to cool down her libido, too.

They ordered their pizza for delivery and adjourned to their respective bathrooms where Josie took a barely warm shower, talking sense to herself as she did. Reminding herself in no uncertain terms that she and Michael were not really engaged. That they were not living together as a couple. And that she had better keep that in mind.

Which she was determined to do. Even though she slipped into her lightest-weight, flowy pajama pants and a loose silk T-shirt with such a wide boat neck that she couldn't wear a bra with it and the slightest movement sent it seductively sliding off her shoulder.

Seduction had nothing to do with her choice of outfit. She told herself it was simply the coolest, softest, most comfortable thing she owned and after a bad day at work and an evening of housecleaning, she deserved it.

She also replaced her makeup and recombed her hair before she padded out of her room on bare feet, vowing that she and Michael really were only going to share a pizza like any two roommates might after cleaning house together.

A simple, platonic pizza.

And nothing more.

Michael was already downstairs, accepting the pizza at the front door when she got there. Josie insisted on at least giving the delivery person a tip since Michael wouldn't let her pay for half of the pie.

They opted for eating at the coffee table in the living room where they sat on the floor, used paper plates and sipped the wine Michael uncorked as Josie took in the sight of him freshly showered, shampooed and shaved. He was wearing clean jeans and a plain, tan crew-necked T-shirt that he filled to the brim with shoulders that went on forever, honed pectorals and bulging biceps that gave her an appetite for more than food.

"So you had a rough day today, huh?" he said as they settled in to eat.

"Pretty rough," she confirmed.

She omitted the fact that she'd found herself noticing babies for the first time since she'd taken the job as the receptionist for Manhattan Multiples and that she'd been thinking about Michael in conjunction with them, and told him only about the threatening letter to Eloise Vale and what had followed.

"What goes on there that has somebody so riled up?" he asked when she'd finished.

"Nothing that you would think would inspire threats. Eloise decided when she had her own triplets that there was a need for support for mothers giving birth to more than one baby at a time, so she founded Manhattan Multiples. We offer a pretty wide range of services, counseling and classes that try to fill the unusual needs and problems of mothers and families in that situation.

There's nothing controversial about it, that's for sure. And nothing that should warrant threats.''

''Are the police thinking you could be in danger?'' Michael asked.

There was concern in his voice and it was nice to hear. Josie explained the recommendations of the police. ''It couldn't have come at a worse time. Finances are already a concern if the mayor cuts our funding. But Eloise said that even if she had to take the money for the upgraded alarm system out of her own pocket, she was still going to do it because she wouldn't risk anything happening to her employees or her clients.''

''Good boss.''

''She really is. She's a very caring, conscientious person. I hate that someone is actually threatening her or that she could be in jeopardy.''

Josie's glass was empty and Michael refilled it, and his own, too.

She accepted the wine but found her appetite— which hadn't been good to begin with—had dwindled even more. So she pushed away what remained of the pizza she'd only been picking at and sat back against the sofa.

''Let's not talk about this anymore,'' she suggested. ''There's really not much that can be done and talking about it makes me jumpy.''

Michael nodded as he polished off his third slice of pizza. He'd apparently had enough, too, because he closed the box, piled their plates on top of it, and took everything into the kitchen.

When he returned he sat beside Josie on the floor in front of the couch, angled in her direction with his thigh only inches from hers. Then he stretched his arm behind her on the cushions.

He didn't touch her but Josie could feel the heat of his body anyway. It was comforting and arousing all at once but she tried to ignore the arousing part as he reached with his free hand for his wineglass.

"Okay. New subject," he announced, lightly clinking his glass against hers. "I've been thinking about our talk the other day—about you growing up in an orphanage and being stubbornly independent and self-sufficient and anti-attachment—"

"Stubbornly?" Josie repeated. "I don't know if I like that term. How about adamantly? Or steadfastly?"

"Okay. Adamantly and steadfastly independent and self-sufficient and anti-attachment," he corrected. "What I was wondering was if that means you've reached the advanced age of twenty-five without ever having had a serious relationship?"

"I have a lot of serious relationships even as we speak," she contended. "With friends. With people I work with…"

"I mean serious romantic relationships," he said, not letting her get away with the dodge.

"I date," she said.

"But not seriously? Are you a love-'em-and-leave-'em person?"

She didn't like the sound of that. "No, I

wouldn't say I'm a love-'em-and-leave-'em person. I just like to keep things light.''

''In other words, you like to keep men at arm's length.''

He wasn't at arm's length now and he certainly hadn't been over the Labor Day weekend.

But Josie didn't point that out to him. ''Why does it have to be one extreme or the other? Either serious or arm's length? I've had fairly long-term, close relationships.''

''*Fairly* long-term, close relationships,'' he repeated. ''How long is *fairly* long-term? And how close is *close?*''

''Close is *close.* Long-term is months. Almost a year once.''

''But what? As soon as you're getting too attached you cut and run?''

''Hey, let's not forget that you're Mister-I'm-Not-Getting-Married-Until-I-Retire. I don't think you have any room to talk.''

He smiled a crooked smile at that. ''I'm not criticizing, just trying to get to know you.''

Josie considered how honest to be with him. How much to let him in. But in the end she opted for being candid. ''It isn't as if I have some quiz I give and if there's attachment developing on either side I run screaming into the night. But yes, I admit that if I start feeling like I might not be able to live without someone, it triggers things in me.''

''Automatically?''

''Pretty much.''

"And no one has snuck in under the radar?"

Josie sipped more of her wine, again thinking over how much she wanted to tell him.

"There was one guy," she finally admitted. "Troy Randall. But he sort of snuck in before the radar was fully up. I met him right after I'd left the orphanage. I was lonely and kind of at odds being on my own for the first time. And there he was. I was waiting tables and he worked in the kitchen as the assistant chef."

"You got close to him," Michael guessed in a gentle tone.

"I did. Too close."

"He was your first." Another guess.

"In so many things," she confirmed. "My first friend outside of the orphanage. The first guy to take me home to meet his family. To be a part of his family. The first person who seemed to care about me not because it was his job, but because he really seemed to care. My first romance. And yes, my *first…*first."

More wine. She needed a bolstering sip to talk about Troy.

"You were with him almost a year?" Michael prodded to get her to go on.

"Just a few days short, as a matter of fact."

"What happened?"

Josie thought about that and suffered the slight twinge of pain the memory could still cause. Then she took a deep breath, sighed it out and said, "He met someone he liked better."

"He cheated on you?"

"He said it wasn't cheating because we didn't have any kind of exclusive commitment."

"After a year together without seeing other people?"

"Well, I know I hadn't seen anyone else and I was under the impression that he hadn't, either. Until then. But he said we were both free agents— that's the way he put it—and that that meant he could do whatever he wanted."

"And he wanted to *do* someone else." Michael's tone was harsh suddenly, almost angry.

"He also said I needed a life. That I was hanging on to him too much. That I was too dependent. And he was probably right. I mean, I really did like him. A lot, or I would never have gone as far as I did. But in retrospect I probably was using him a little too much as a crutch, too. Like I said, I was on my own for the first time and—"

"And the first person you trusted outside of the orphanage abandoned you the same way your parents did. Or, actually, in a worse way because he did it willingly."

Josie laughed a bit wryly. "Are we doing armchair analysis now?"

Michael finished his wine and set the glass on the coffee table. "He did, didn't he?"

"It wasn't as if I was his responsibility. He wasn't obligated to me. He was just a guy I worked with—"

"Who took you under his wing and made you

believe he really cared about you and slept with you and then turned around and slept with someone else.''

''It taught me a good lesson,'' Josie insisted without refuting Michael's summary.

''He taught you to be even more afraid to get attached to anyone.''

''It taught me that I really did need to be independent. That I had to take care of myself. And from that I learned that I *like* being independent and taking care of myself. That I like being free.''

''Seems to me that losing your parents when you were so little taught you that fate could be cruel and snatch away people you love, and then this jerk let you know people could be just as cruel. And maybe when you put the two things together, being free is just a way of protecting yourself.''

''Ooo, we *are* playing armchair analysis,'' Josie joked, not taking what he was saying too seriously.

''It just seems to me that if you never let anyone get too close for too long you're going to look back someday and regret it because all you'll be looking back on is a life strung with a million different jobs and a million different people you've only had superficial relationships with. And there you'll be, alone with nothing but Pip's latest successor.''

The big dog was curled in the corner of the living room and his ears perked up when he heard his name.

But when no other attention was paid him, the

bull mastiff stood as if he was miffed at being disturbed for no reason and went into the kitchen.

"I'll still have my poetry. That's the constant in my life," Josie said then, putting her glass on the coffee table, too.

"Poetry isn't going to tie your shoes when you're too old to bend over and do it yourself."

"Ah, well, a good portion of being self-sufficient is anticipating things like that. I'll wear slip-ons."

Michael laughed. "You know, it might be different if you were no fun, but you're too terrific not to share it with other people. Not to have kids who could be just as terrific. You're wasted on Pip."

"I beg your pardon. Pip appreciates me," she said, pretending affront when in fact it pleased her a lot to know he thought that of her.

"Pip doesn't appreciate you enough," Michael countered.

Something had changed in his voice suddenly. And in the way he was looking at her. His green eyes were softer, more entreating.

"I mean it, Josie," he said then, much more soberly. "You're sweet and funny and kind and smart and talented and a hundred other things that make you special. Too special not to have a full life in every way. You deserve love and commitment and a husband and a family and a dozen grandchildren who adore you, too. Don't deny yourself just for the sake of avoiding a hurt that might not happen.''

''I could say the same to you,'' she pointed out in a gentle tone of her own.

Michael smiled, conceding that there was some merit to that. ''So we're both idiots?''

Josie laughed but it came out a breathy, sexy sort of chuckle. ''I guess so.''

It was almost as if reaching that conclusion bound them together. Their eyes seemed locked, searching for answers, maybe. Making that connection that kept happening between them against all odds and when Josie least expected it.

But there it was again and all thought, all reason, just faded into oblivion along with the rest of the world, leaving only Josie, only Michael...

Josie didn't know when his arm had come around her from the couch cushions. When his hand had woven its way into her hair.

She didn't know when her own hand had drifted to his knee where it was bent and touching the side of her thigh.

She didn't even know how much time passed after they'd stopped talking and begun looking into each other's eyes.

She only knew that when he dipped in slowly to kiss her it seemed like exactly what he was supposed to do.

That first kiss was brief, interrupted so he could start again, the second time with his head angled to the left rather than to the right. So they could both be more comfortable.

Josie raised her hands to the sides of his face, smooth now and giving off only a hint of the scent of his aftershave.

His free hand reached for her wrist, following a path along her forearm to her elbow, to her upper arm, leaving tiny shards of delight in his wake before he wrapped both arms around her and pulled her to him.

And oh, but it was nice to be back in those arms!

He deepened the kiss. Then deepened it still more. Parting his lips and waiting for her to part hers, too.

Which she did. Heaven help her, she knew somewhere in the recesses of her brain that she shouldn't, but she did anyway. She opened her mouth to his tongue when it came to greet hers, meeting it without any coyness at all. With eagerness, in fact.

She slid her hands to the nape of his neck, up into his hair and then down again until she filled them with the rock-hard strength of his back, finding familiar territory, reveling in the opportunity to feel once more what she'd thought never to glory in again.

Her nipples tightened into delirious little knots against his chest, nudging him to let him know they were there. There and yearning for his attention through the thin fabric of her shirt as mouths went on feasting and everything inside her seemed to come alive.

Then, while one of Michael's hands stayed to brace her, to hold her, the other began a slow massage, a caress of more than just her back. Of the side of her neck. Of her shoulder. Of her collarbone...

Anticipation grew in her as that hand drifted downward until he found her breast.

Josie arched her spine and a tiny, barely audible moan rumbled in her throat at that initial contact that felt so good and yet only made her want more.

Or less, actually. Less between them.

Michael seemed to know what she craved. Just as he'd seemed to know all through the Labor Day weekend. That hand abandoned her breast only long enough to find its way under her shirt. To enclose her breast again, this time in the warmth of bare flesh against bare flesh.

If her nipple had been hard before, it was nothing compared to the pebble it became in the center of his palm as his adept fingers kneaded that oh-so-sensitive globe.

So sensitive...

So sensitive she could hardly believe it. More than it had ever been before. Better than it had ever been before.

It was almost too good to bear and she was lost in sensations that made her writhe, that rushed through her like a raging river.

She plunged her own hands under his shirt, desperate for even more of his naked skin as his mouth continued to plunder hers and his hand worked those wonders at her breast.

Yet even having her bare hand on his skin, and his on hers, wasn't enough. She wanted more. She wanted to be naked in his arms. She wanted him naked against her. She wanted his hands everywhere. His mouth everywhere. She wanted it all. All of him. And she wanted it so much it almost hurt...

Maybe that was what finally made her realize that she was getting carried away again. As carried away as she had over that weekend. With the same man she'd sworn not to ever get carried away with again...

Josie forced herself to tear her mouth from his, leaning backward at the same time to break his hold on her altogether, breathing deeply, her eyes still closed from their kiss.

"Just friends. Just roommates..." She whispered the agreement they seemed to keep making—and breaking—as she fought to catch her breath and regain some self-control.

After a few minutes she opened her eyes, struggling for sanity, for reality, finding only Michael's breathtakingly handsome face there in front of her, his expression as dazed as she felt.

"Right. Just friends. Just roommates," he repeated. "We keep forgetting that, don't we?"

"Just friends. Just roommates. No sex," Josie said again, reminding herself as much as him.

But his smile was so devilishly delicious it was irresistible. "That wasn't sex," he said as if the words alone could change what had just happened.

"It was close enough," Josie insisted.

He moaned slightly and shook his head in what looked a little like agony. "Not by a long shot," he murmured.

Josie couldn't help laughing and she knew that that charm of his was what made it so difficult to remember why she couldn't give in to this. To him.

"Are you working tomorrow?" she asked to put things back on the level they should never have left.

"I am. Ordinarily I work four twenty-four-hour shifts and then have four days in a row off. But like I told you the other night, we're two men short."

"It's probably for the best," she said emphatically. "Not that you're two men short. But that you'll be there instead of here," she qualified, worrying after the fact how that might have sounded.

But before she made anything worse, she got up from the floor and went into the kitchen to let Pip out for the last time of the night so she could escape to her bed.

When the big dog had spent a few minutes in the yard, she let him in again and returned to the living room. Michael was still sitting where he'd been before and Josie had to fight the strongest urge not to just sit back down beside him and pick up where they'd left off.

"Good night," she said simply enough, concealing what she was struggling with inside.

Michael didn't answer that simply, though. Instead he said, "You know, this would all be a lot easier if I didn't like you so damn much."

Josie couldn't help smiling at that. Or being warmed from the inside out by him saying it.

"Yeah, you could make it easier on me by being a creep," she countered.

His chuckle was wry. "I'll see what I can do."

"Thanks. I'd appreciate it," she said before she actually did go up the stairs to her room.

But when she finally got to the safety of it, it wasn't really much of an escape at all.

Because she'd brought with her so many unquenched, forbidden desires that she couldn't sleep and ended up tossing and turning all night.

Tossing and turning and battling to keep from crossing that single hallway to Michael's room.

Chapter Seven

Michael didn't like to be in a rush before work so he always got up earlier than he needed to. Which was why he was showered, shaved, dressed and ready to go half an hour before it was time to leave the house Tuesday morning.

But unlike other mornings when he drank his coffee at the kitchen table while he read the newspaper, this morning he took his steaming cup and went into the living room to sit on the couch.

Right next to the spot he and Josie had leaned against the previous night.

He knew it was a dumb thing to do. As it was he hadn't been able to stop replaying the events of the last evening in his head a hundred times. And

now there he was, sitting and staring at the scene
of the crime, reliving it all again.

Not that holding Josie, kissing her, touching her,
had been a crime. Nothing that good could be
criminal. It was just that being where it had happened made the whole thing even more vivid. And
the more vivid it was, the tougher it was to put out
of his mind the way he knew he should. The
tougher it was not to want to do it again. Which
was why, even though it might not technically be
returning to the scene of a crime, it was still a
dumb thing to indulge in.

But dumb or not, he stayed sitting there, staring
at the exact place they'd been, picturing every moment, reliving every detail. Recalling the feel of
her in his arms. Remembering what it was like to
kiss her. Tasting again the sweetness of her lips.
Smelling the clean scent of her hair…

In his mind he felt her response to every touch
of his hands. He heard the tiny, involuntary sounds
she'd made. He could feel again the pure, unadul-
terated pleasure of having her hands on him. Soft
hands. On his face. His neck. Against his back.

It had all just felt so damn amazing….

He realized suddenly that somewhere in the process of reliving it he'd actually laid his palm to the
place on the sofa cushions where their backs had
rested. Hell, he was even caressing it. Kneading it
a little. The way he'd caressed and kneaded—

Okay, knock it off, he commanded, cutting short
the wandering of his own thoughts.

What was he, some adolescent boy who couldn't control his own thoughts?

That notion made him laugh slightly at himself. Because what was going on with him when it came to Josie really was a lot like what he remembered of a teenage crush he'd had on a red-haired girl who had sat in front of him in algebra. He hadn't been able to concentrate on anything but her. He'd spent hours daydreaming about her. Fantasizing about her. Being obsessed with her. He'd even brushed his hand against the back of her chair on his way out of class just to be able to touch the place she'd been.

There were elements of all that in what was going on with him in regard to Josie.

And wasn't that just what he needed? he thought facetiously. To go through adolescence a second time? Terrific.

Although he might actually be better off if that was *all* that was involved here, he thought. Because what had him really worried was that he didn't merely have some kind of teenage crush on her. That there might be more to it than an adolescent infatuation.

He genuinely liked Josie. A lot. Enough that it had actually stabbed him to think about the way she'd grown up. It had made him want to make it up to her somehow, the way he would have wanted to make up for something bad happening to someone he cared about.

Plus, he enjoyed her company so much that every minute he was away from her he actually counted the hours until he could see her again. He'd refused to meet friends for drinks, to go to the movies, because nothing appealed to him as much as being alone with Josie. He'd even turned down free tickets to see the Giants just so he could rush home to her. Not to mention that he hated it when they ended those evenings he did get to spend with her, that no evening seemed long enough. And then he went to sleep imagining her in the room across from his, picturing her curled up in bed.

In bed…

That was another thing—there was no denying that he wanted her. In the worst way. Or the best way. But either way, he wanted her more than he'd ever wanted any woman. More than he'd wanted the red-haired girl. And that was saying something.

But none of that changed anything.

Just because he liked Josie, just because he had more fun with her than with any woman he knew, just because he wanted her as much as a drowning man wanted a lifeline, that didn't mean he could run with it. Not and still be a firefighter. Not when there were other things as vivid in his mind as what he and Josie had shared the night before.

Things like answering the door when the fire chief had come to tell them the worst had happened.

Things like standing by his mother's side through the funeral service.

Things like sports events and camping trips with friends and their fathers when he didn't have one.

Things like finding his mother crying for his father long after his father was gone.

He couldn't put Josie through that. In fact, the thought of putting anyone through it had always been like a bucket of cold water thrown on him to bring him to his senses. Now, knowing Josie the way he did, picturing her, specifically, in that position, had more impact.

Josie, who was so full of life, so happy, made unbearably sad because fate might have other plans for him the way it had had for his father? That wasn't an image he could stand. Especially now that he knew she'd already suffered a loss like that. When he knew how deep an impact it had had on her.

Pip came down the stairs just then, his heavy paws thumping on each step and pulling Michael's gaze from the sofa to see if Josie was coming with him. Hoping Josie was coming with him...

But she wasn't. Only the big honey-colored dog joined him, crossing to Michael to nudge his leg for attention.

"How'd you get out?" he asked as if Pip might answer. "Did your mom leave the door cracked just enough for you to get it open?"

Pip licked his hand and then plopped his square head atop Michael's knee.

"I'll take that as a yes," Michael said, petting the animal behind the ears.

And that was when it occurred to Michael that he was being dumb in more ways than just sitting there picturing what he and Josie had done the previous evening. He was also being dumb in thinking that taking this relationship with Josie any further was completely up to him when she'd made it clear that she didn't want any serious involvement, either. When she'd made it clear that Pip was the only long-term object of her affection. That she was absolutely not interested in any kind of attachment to anyone *but* Pip.

"She'd get a good laugh out of this, wouldn't she?" he said quietly to the mastiff. "Here I am being noble about not wanting to put her through losing me and she doesn't even want me. Well, at least not for anything serious."

And why did that make him feel some pretty sharp pangs?

Maybe he wasn't only dumb. Maybe he was crazy, too.

He stood then and said, "Come on, I'll let you out before I leave."

The dog loped along behind him to the back door. Michael opened it for him and finished the last of his coffee standing there until Pip came back in.

"I better get going," he told the dog as he locked the door after him.

Michael rinsed his coffee cup and put it in the dishwasher. Then he and Pip returned to the living room where Michael picked up the duffel bag that held his change of clothes and the other necessities he brought back and forth to work.

As he did, Pip headed up the stairs again and Michael suffered a wave of envy. In spite of everything, he would have liked to pad up those steps to Josie's room, too.

"You're hopeless," he muttered disgustedly to himself—and about himself.

But even as he went out the front door and into the early morning September sunshine, he was still imagining Josie in her bed. Asleep. The way he'd seen her over Labor Day weekend.

And, in spite of all he'd just reminded himself of, he would have given just about anything at that moment to be slipping into that bed with her. To be waking her with soft kisses. With tender touches. With his body pressed against hers to let her know how much he wanted her...

"Definitely hopeless," he repeated as he set off down the street. "Hopeless, dumb and crazy."

"Josie? Do you have a minute before you leave?"

Josie was halfway out the door of Manhattan Multiples for lunch on Wednesday when Leah Simpson stopped her. She *didn't* have a minute to spare since she was meeting her former roommate, but she stopped anyway.

"Is it important?" she asked the previously homeless woman Eloise had rescued but who no one still knew much about.

"I don't know. I just went into Allison's office to bring her those papers you wanted her to have and I think she might be sick or something."

The day Allison had been short-tempered with the reporter had not been an isolated incident.

Allison had been acting strangely ever since. She was moody. Distracted. She seemed to snap at every little thing. Josie was beginning to worry about her.

"What's wrong?" she inquired of Leah.

"Allison's head was down on her desk and I'm sure she was sleeping—I had to call her name three times before she sat up and she did it with a jolt. But she got all mad at me when I apologized for waking her. She said she hadn't been sleeping. But she doesn't look so good."

Out of concern for Allison, Josie turned back into the office. "I'll poke my nose in and make sure she's okay. Go have your lunch. You look like you can use a little rest, too."

That was true enough. Leah was in the third trimester of her pregnancy with triplets and it wasn't easy for her to be working even though everyone at Manhattan Multiples made sure she took plenty of breaks.

"I do need to get off my feet for a minute or two," Leah said as Josie went to her desk and set down her purse.

"Go ahead," Josie encouraged as she picked up the phone to make a quick call to Sharon to tell her she was going to be late. Then she headed for Allison's office.

Despite the fact that Leah had been there only moments before, when Josie reached Allison's open door she found her as Leah had described— head on her desk, eyes closed, and not responding to her name until Josie said it a second time.

Then Allison sat up as if Josie had frightened her. There was an imprint of her desk blotter on the side of her face as evidence that she'd been napping for some time.

"Are you okay?" Josie asked, stepping into the office.

"Fine," Allison said curtly. "Why does everyone keep asking me that?"

"It just isn't like you to spend your lunch hour snoozing. If you aren't feeling well, you could go home, you know. I'll cover for you."

"I feel fine. I'm just a little tired," Allison said, apparently giving up her attempt to convince anyone that she wasn't napping.

"Are you having problems sleeping at night?" Josie asked. "Because when I have insomnia I use aroma therapy and it almost always—"

"I'm not having trouble sleeping. I think I could sleep 'round the clock lately. It just isn't easy going to law school at night and working all day."

"I'm sure it isn't," Josie said, refraining from pointing out that Allison had been keeping up with her classes and work without falling asleep at her desk before. "Maybe you should just take a day to yourself, sleep in until noon, lay around and watch old movies and eat junk food—recharge your batteries. You have the time coming and one day won't hurt anything."

Poor Allison suddenly switched from hostility to looking as if she were on the verge of tears, confusing Josie even more.

Allison did accept her suggestion, though. "I

might do that. Maybe I'll take Friday. That would give me a three-day weekend."

"Good idea. I'll make sure everything around here is taken care of. Pamper yourself."

Allison nodded but she still seemed so distraught and so worn out that Josie wondered if Friday would be soon enough for her.

"How about lunch? I'm on my way to meet a friend but we'd love to have you join us."

"No, thanks. I brought a sandwich."

"How about a goody? Can I bring you something back?" Josie offered, hoping to lift her spirits with chocolate the way she had on Friday when Allison had been out of sorts.

Only this time Allison seemed too down for even that to perk her up. "I don't think so," she said. "But if you'd close that door on your way out, I'd appreciate it."

Josie had the feeling that Allison wanted the door closed so she could go back to sleep, but she didn't say anything about it. What Allison did on her lunch hour wasn't anyone's business but Allison's.

"Sure."

Josie stepped out of the office and had the door partially shut before her concerns caused her to stop and say, "Remember, if you want to talk or there's anything I can do—"

"I remember. Thanks," Allison said halfheartedly. But she didn't take her up on the offer. She just stared at Josie until Josie got the hint that she really didn't want to say any more and closed the door the rest of the way.

"See?" Leah whispered when Josie rejoined her in the reception area. "Something is up with her, isn't it?"

"She doesn't seem quite herself," Josie answered. "But we all have times when we're a little off our game. Let's just be patient with her."

"You don't think we should tell Eloise?"

"I think Eloise has enough on her mind right now and if Allison wants her to know something is going on, it's more Allison's place to say it than ours."

"Okay," Leah agreed. "Then I guess I'll put my feet up and eat my lunch."

"And I guess I'll go meet my friend for mine."

But even as Josie left the office she cast a glance back at Allison's door, wondering what exactly was going on with the other woman.

Josie and Sharon had barely finished ordering salads for lunch when Sharon squinted her eyes at Josie in an assessing stare.

"Hmm. You look tired. Does that mean you haven't been getting enough sleep because you're spending every night making mad, passionate love with Michael?"

"I haven't seen you since I moved out of the apartment and the best you can say to me is that I look tired?" Josie asked, ignoring her former roommate's question but not taking offense to it.

Sharon seemed to study her closer. "Tired but

not happy-tired,'' she concluded. "That must mean you're losing sleep because you *want* to be making mad, passionate love with him and aren't letting yourself.''

Josie laughed at her friend's insight and debated about whether or not to deny the accusation. When she made her decision, she did a comical banging of her forehead on the table in mock distress and said, "Oh, boy, do I want to.''

Sharon laughed, too. "So do it!''

Josie sat up straight again and said a resigned, "I can't.''

"Uh-oh. Isn't he interested?''

"It isn't that. I'm pretty sure he is interested. He's kissed me. And then some. But I haven't let it go all the way again.''

"Oh, come on! Where's that free spirit? Where's that grabbing-life-with-both-hands attitude?''

There were a number of things on Michael that Josie would have liked to grab with both hands but she didn't say that. Instead she said, "Remaining a free spirit requires me not to sleep with him because it would put me at risk of getting tied down.''

"Oh, bull. You're just afraid. But I thought the attraction between the two of you would be strong enough to get you over that.''

"I'm not afraid,'' Josie claimed feebly.

"You are *so* afraid. You're terrified. Of his job. Of making a commitment—''

"Well, you were afraid of his mother, so you don't have any room to talk."

"True! I was definitely terrified of his mother," Sharon acknowledged good-naturedly. But she still didn't let Josie off the hook. "But I wasn't losing sleep over it and you are. Because you really like this guy and that's why you should give him a chance. And another tumble."

"There's nothing *not* to like about him," Josie said as if that somehow diminished the importance of it when that was part of the problem.

"And you're so hot for him you can hardly stand it."

"I can stand it," Josie lied.

But apparently she hadn't lied convincingly enough because Sharon ignored it. "I thought it was part of being a bohemian to live in the moment? And in this moment you want this guy so much you can't keep your hands off him. So I say, why not go with it? What real harm would there be in that?"

It was a question Josie was asking herself more and more. Still she said, "There could be a lot of harm in that."

"Or a lot of good. So what if he's in a dangerous line of work? The vast majority of people who do it go all the way through their careers without anything awful happening to them. And as for your phobia about attachment? Hey, if it's with the right person, attachment is a good thing and you don't feel tied down. Besides," Sharon added with a sly twist to her smile, "you aren't attached to the guy yet, right?"

"No, I'm not attached to him yet."

"Then you could sleep with him again as a test to see how it rates with that weekend you spent with him. Who knows? You might end up wondering what all the fuss was about in the first place."

Josie laughed again. "You think I should sleep with him just to see if I'm remembering right?"

"It's one reason."

Josie rolled her eyes. "I think it's better to just keep things platonic."

"I never thought I'd see it," Sharon said, shaking her head.

"What?"

"Our little free bird turning conservative."

But Josie refused to take the goad seriously as the waitress brought their food.

The day ended up being a long, tiring one for Josie. But her weariness was cured on the way home from work by just the thought that Michael might be there, that she might get to spend the evening with him. The mere possibility wiped away all the fatigue that had caused her friend to know she'd been up nights thinking about the man who was supposed to be nothing more than her roommate.

She could hear water running in the kitchen when she went into the brownstone. She hooked the strap of her purse over the newel post on the banister at the foot of the stairs and followed the sound before she'd even kicked off her shoes—that was how eager she was to see him. And she didn't waste a single thought on analyzing it or fighting it, she just followed her heart's desire and went looking for him.

Michael was at the sink, all right, but the moment Josie saw him she knew something was up. His back was to her—his wonderful back with its broad shoulders that did a graceful V dive to his narrow waist and gold-medal buns. But he was still in the dark pants and the T-shirt emblazoned with the letters FDNY across the breadth of those shoulders. The clothes were one form of his uniform and since his shift had ended early that morning he should have changed out of them long ago.

"I'm home," Josie announced from the doorway that connected the kitchen to the living room.

Michael barely glanced back at her. "Hi," he said, returning to what he was doing.

But even that was enough to convey a sense of tension emanating from him.

Pip was sitting patiently on the floor by his side so it gave Josie the excuse to join them and get closer. She crossed the kitchen, saying, "Hello, Pippy, did you miss me today?"

Pip wagged his tail but he didn't budge from Michael's side and for some reason Josie had the impression there was almost something protective in the stance. But that didn't make any sense. Until she went from petting her dog to peering around Michael to see what he was doing.

That was also when she realized Michael was a touch on the grimy side. That there were smudges of dirt on his shirt and even on his whisker-shadowed face. And that he was washing a yellowish-orange discoloration off his left forearm, being careful to avoid a row of black stitches in his skin.

When she saw that and realized what it was, all pretense went out the window and Josie said, "What happened?"

"Bad day," Michael answered tersely.

He didn't offer any more than that, though, and because it wasn't easy to have a conversation over running water, Josie waited while he finished.

When he had, he turned off the faucet, grabbed a towel to blot his arm and said, "Tell me you don't have any plans but to sit around here tonight."

Oh, yeah, he was definitely tense.

"Sitting around here tonight was my plan," she said.

"Good. I can't tell you how much I was hoping that would be the case and we could just maybe have a quiet dinner together and chill out."

Josie did make an attempt not to let both the idea of spending the evening with him and the fact that he seemed to want it so desperately himself thrill her as much as it did. She also decided to postpone delving into whatever it was that was going on with him until he'd had a chance to mellow.

So instead of pursuing the subject of his bad day—which seemed to have been far worse than hers—she said, "When I got home from work yesterday I found that two steaks and a bowl of potato salad had manifested themselves in the fridge—''

"My mother will do that every now and then— use her key to come in while I'm gone and leave food.''

"Ah, I thought she had the aura of the food fairy about her. Anyway, I make a mean steak. So, what if I change my clothes and you go up and shower, and by the time you have, I've broiled the steaks?''

Michael was finished drying off his arm and he turned away from the sink, letting his hips rest against the edge of the countertop and his eyes settle on her. "That sounds great," he said as if it somehow made him feel relieved. Then he added, "I really need this.''

She pretended to misunderstand in order to make a joke and lighten the tone. "You really need a good steak and some potato salad?''

It worked because he finally cracked a smile, albeit a weak one. "No. What I really need is time with you," he said simply enough before he pushed off the counter and left her standing there alone in the kitchen.

Alone and awash in warm fuzzy feelings.

Michael didn't seem to want to talk about his day as they ate, either. He guided the conversation to Josie's work, wanting to know if there had been any more threats made against Eloise or Manhattan Multiples, and if the new security system had been installed.

Josie assumed he wasn't ready to talk about

what was on his mind, so she told him yes, the security system was in the process of being installed, all the while trying to keep the mood as upbeat as possible.

After dinner they did the dishes together and then Michael suggested they each have a second bottle of the imported beer they'd had with dinner.

Josie agreed, checked on Pip who as happily chasing squirrels in the backyard, and she and Michael took their beers into the living room.

When they got there, Michael sat low in the center of the sofa so he could rest his head on the back. Then he put his bare feet up on the coffee table, crossing them at the ankles.

Josie sat beside him, facing him and curling her legs to one side and underneath her. She'd changed into a pair of loose-fitting Capri pants and a peasant blouse that opened from the round neckline down about six-inches. A navy blue ribbon laced the edges of the opening together but the ribbon was untied and the ends dangled down the front of the shirt. Her feet were bare, too, and it suddenly struck her that there was something subtly intimate about the casualness of the situation.

But she tried to ignore it.

"So, are you going to tell me about your day now?" she asked.

The question alone put creases between Michael's brows and before he answered it one way or another he took a long pull off his beer.

Once he had, he repeated, "Bad day."

And that was it. He didn't offer any more.

But Josie's curiosity was too intense by then to let it drop so she tried another tack. "What happened to your arm?"

He'd showered, shaved and changed into a pair of age-softened jeans and a plain white crew-necked T-shirt. The sleeves of the T-shirt were pushed up to his elbows, baring both forearms, and his gaze settled on the gash on his left arm, covered by a gauze bandage now.

"All part of the bad day," he said.

Josie thought she might scream if he didn't quit stalling and give her an actual answer, but rather than ask him anything else, she merely let silence fall, hoping that might spur him to say more.

After a few minutes and another drink of his beer, the tactic worked because Michael said, "We had a slow night last night. I actually got a full eight hours' sleep. I figured I was coming home today to do some yardwork, putter around the house. But about an hour before the end of my shift this morning we got a call. An accident involving a car and a truck. The driver of the car was pinned in the wreck and they needed the Jaws of Life to get him out."

"The Jaws of Life? That's something the fire department does, too?" Josie asked, never having considered who actually operated them.

"Right," Michael confirmed. "Actually, when it comes to most of the dirty work even outside of fires, we get the call."

He took another swig of his beer before he continued. "Anyway, we got to the scene and it was

bad. The guy had left for work like any other day
and this had happened two blocks from his house.
He was in and out of consciousness, in a lot of
pain. We were working as fast as we could, emergency medical techs were on the scene but they
couldn't get a handle on the extent of his injuries
enough to do much more than give him some pain
medication while he was still stuck in that heap of
metal. Then, to make matters worse, the guy's wife
and kids showed up—''

"How did that happen?" Josie asked, cringing
at just the thought of the man's family entering the
picture.

"The wife was driving the kids to school. She
recognized the car and stopped. She was hysteri-
cal—how could she be anything else? The kids
were a mess—crying for their dad—''

"Were they close enough to watch?"

"No, the police kept them outside the perime-
ters, but…" Michael shook his head and his expression let Josie know just how horrific the memory was. "We could still hear them calling to the
guy, crying, begging him to be all right and us to
help him." Another shake of the head. "I just
couldn't work as fast as any of us wished I could."

"Was the family there the whole time?"

"The police got the mother to agree to let the
kids be taken home by a neighbor and told her she
had to go to the hospital they planned to bring her
husband to, to wait for him there. But the guy had
heard enough for it to register that they'd been
nearby and even after the police cleared the family

out, he would come to and call for them…" Michael took a deep breath and breathed it out hard. "It was bad."

"I can't imagine," Josie said quietly. "How long did it take to get him out?"

"It was after noon."

"But was he all right? I mean, did he make it?"

Michael shook his head again, this time in answer. "When we finally got him free, we discovered that the pressure of the steering wheel had kept the bleeding to a minimum. But once that was removed, he was in even more trouble. The EMTs worked on him the whole way to the hospital but he bled out before we got there."

"*We?* You rode in the ambulance with him?"

Michael pointed his beer at his injured arm. "I'd cut myself on some of the metal getting him out, so they packed me into the ambulance to take to the hospital, too. For the stitches. So yeah, I got to take the full ride on this one, beginning to end. I was even just in the next room when the wife was told that her husband had died."

"Oh, Michael, I'm so sorry," Josie said, placing a hand to his uninjured arm and her brow to the side of his head.

"Like I said, bad day."

She hadn't thought about the consequences of touching him. She'd only thought to comfort him. But the spot where her hand connected with his arm, even the spot where their heads met, seemed to come alive to Josie suddenly.

She sat up and took her hand away, but apparently Michael didn't want to lose all contact with her because the moment she had, he took her hand in his.

"Thanks for this tonight," he said, smiling a little. "I really didn't want to just hang around here alone. And it was nice to be pampered, too."

"Wait till you get my bill," she joked, fighting the tiny shards of light that were shooting up her arm just because he was holding her hand.

"No matter what you're charging me, it's worth it," he countered. But even though she knew he was kidding, too, there was something else in his voice. In the air all around them, in fact. Something that only increased the sense of intimacy Josie had felt when they'd first come into the living room.

Michael pulled his feet off the coffee table then and set his beer bottle there instead. When he sat back again he didn't slouch down to rest his head. He sat straight and angled in Josie's direction.

"You do something to me," he said, his gaze on their joined hands.

"What do I do to you?"

"I can't explain it. Something good, though. Really good. I was sitting at that hospital this afternoon, waiting to be released, and all I could think was that everything would be okay as soon as I was home with you. That just seeing you would make things better."

"I don't know how much better I made anything," she said. "You've been pretty down all night."

"Yeah, but I *feel* a lot better now," he assured her, sounding as if he actually did since there was a sexy sort of edge to his tone and a much more relaxed smile on his face.

Josie knew right then that she should withdraw her hand from his. That she should put some distance between them. That she should probably even say good-night and go up to her room. She'd helped him get through the evening. She'd gotten him to talk over the awful experience of his day. And now that things were changing between them, now that she could tell they were entering that territory they'd toyed with too many times already, she knew she should retreat before anything came of it.

But she couldn't. She just couldn't make herself. He was right, this was nice. Very nice. Sitting there with him. Near to him. Having that big hand of his encasing hers, rubbing hers with feathery strokes of his thumb. The last thing she wanted to do was to put an end to any of it.

And that was when Sharon's words from lunch flashed through her mind again. That was when Josie began to think about living in the moment. About *having* this moment. About allowing herself everything that came out of this moment. This moment with Michael. About just giving in to what she really, really wanted...

So when he raised his other hand to the side of her neck, when he pulled her nearer, when his mouth met hers just then, she didn't shy away. She didn't say no. She didn't stop him or do any of the things she knew she should do. Instead she silenced all the thoughts that shouted caution and answered the pressure of his lips on hers to kiss him back.

She wasn't sure if it was the somber mood that had prevailed all evening or the fact that they'd waded through it together, but that kiss was different right from the start. It was deeper and more powerful, along with being so hot it sizzled.

Then Michael ended it to take her beer and set it on the coffee table with his, returning to wrap his arms around her and to pull her close, recapturing her mouth with lips that were parted.

Josie answered in kind, sliding her arms under his to press her palms to his back, opening her mouth and welcoming his tongue when it came to court hers. To explore, to cling, to taste, to torment and taunt and tease.

"I want you, Josie," Michael said during a split-second break between more kisses.

"I want you, too," she confessed.

And that seemed to be all there was to it—a craving for one another so overwhelming it swept them away.

Michael stopped kissing her and stood, grasping her hand to urge her to her feet, too, then taking her with him up the stairs to his room—that room she remembered so well from their weekend.

And if ever there was a time for Josie to rethink her decision, it was now.

But she didn't. The only thing on her mind was

that she was going to be with him. The way she had been before. The way she wanted to be now.

Michael took her to the side of his big bed without turning on a light, leaving the room dusted only in moonglow. He swung her into his arms once again to continue kissing her as he had been downstairs.

Josie let her head fall back, offering her mouth to his, meeting his tongue lightly, playfully, artlessly, as she returned her palms to his back, this time sliding them underneath his shirt so she could savor that first feel of his warm flesh.

He followed her lead, grabbing hold of the hem of her shirt and slowly bringing it upward, deserting her lips only long enough to pull the peasant blouse over her head.

The lacy bra she wore didn't offer much covering and she wasn't about to be the only one exposed, so she mimicked his actions, divesting him of his shirt, too, as he kissed the side of her neck, working his way upward, nibbling on her jawbone.

Michael unhooked her bra next, freeing her breasts to his naked chest when he enfolded her in his arms again, indulging in that simple sensation of skin to skin as her nipples became tiny knots nudging into him.

It felt wonderful. But it wasn't enough. Not for Josie, not when her body was coming alive with needs that had been too long suppressed.

She wrapped her arms high up around him, around his shoulders, freeing the path to her breasts.

But he didn't take the route she'd exposed. He didn't send his hands to her sides. He didn't slowly come forward and take what she was offering. Instead he slipped lower himself, kissing a trail down to the hollow of her throat, down the center of her breastbone.

He dropped one conciliatory kiss to the very tip of her nipple and then took her other breast into the warm, wet cavern of his mouth before he'd even touched it with his hand. And that and the fact that once again all the sensations of her engorged flesh were heightened, made a faint, primitive sound roll from her throat.

Then he was gone, leaving warm moisture to air dry as he swept her up into his arms and took her with him onto the bed.

He put her on her back and settled himself above her, his lower half following the fluid lines of hers while he braced his upper half on his elbows and held her head lovingly between his hands to kiss her again. A kiss this time that was like a first kiss. Full of awe. Of wonder. Of tenderness.

He kissed her upper lip and then her lower. He kissed her chin. Her cheeks. The tip of her nose and each of her eyes in turn. He kissed the side of her neck and then the hollow, lingering there to bathe her skin in the warm sweetness of his breath before he returned to her mouth in hungry, hungry kisses, as if all of Labor Day weekend and what had happened since then had only whetted his appetite and left him famished for this, now.

Then he rolled to her side instead, holding her

close, tight, with only one arm while his other hand went traveling from her thigh upward to her rear end where he pressed her hips to him and let her feel how much he wanted her before he brought his hand higher still, finally cupping her breast in that warm palm. Kneading. Discovering how little was required to turn her nipple to granite, to make her writhe with pure pleasure.

Once more he took her breast into his mouth, trailing his hands down to rid her of her Capri pants and undies in a sensuous undressing.

Shedding his own jeans caused an interruption in the magic his mouth was working at her breast but it was worth it to get to look at him. At his glorious body bathed in moonlight. At the long, hard length of him. At a magnificence that nearly stole her breath before he slipped on a condom and came back to her, crawling up the length of her to press steamy kisses everywhere along the way to finding her mouth with his again.

Only his hands went exploring now. Wonderful hands. On her breasts. Tugging at her nipples. Teasing her navel with tiny circles around it. Dropping lower still. Reaching the tender inside of her legs. Moving upward to that juncture where they met.

She couldn't help the half sigh, half moan that escaped at that. Any more than she could keep herself from finally reaching for him. From taking that steely staff into her own hands and relearning the heat, the strength of it, driving him as wild as he was driving her.

Until neither of them could bear it a moment longer.

Michael rose above her once more and Josie opened to him so he could fit himself between her thighs and ease into her in one silky movement that felt so good her back arched off the mattress. So good it was better than anything she remembered of Labor Day weekend. Never had anything felt that incredible.

Then he slid more deeply into her, pulling out again, coming in again. Slowly. Tantalizingly.

Josie met and matched him, raising her hips into him when he pushed into her. Retreating just enough when he retreated. Going back for more. Gaining speed. Losing caution. Faster and faster, they moved together, he into her, her meeting him, in a perfect rhythm. Racing. Striving. Straining for that ultimate goal that finally burst inside Josie, blinding her with a white-hot explosion that held her in its miraculous grip, that stopped time and breath, suspending her in unequaled bliss exactly when Michael reached his own climax, exactly when every muscle in his magnificent body tensed and he plunged more deeply into her than she'd thought possible…

Until they both crossed over that crest to descend back into reality.

Inch by inch he let his weight rest atop her as they caught their breaths. As pulses settled into more normal beats. As bodies stayed melded, united, splendidly satiated.

Only after a while like that did Michael rise up

again enough to kiss her forehead. Then he rolled onto his back, taking her to lie beside him, to use his massive chest as her pillow.

And as Josie rested there, lingering between being awake and asleep in his arms, in the afterglow of lovemaking that felt as if it had joined more than their bodies, she knew why it was that she hadn't been able to forget him no matter how hard she'd tried.

What she didn't know, was where they would go from here.

Chapter Eight

Two things woke Josie bright and early the next morning—sunlight streaming in through the window and the telephone ringing from the nightstand beside the bed.

Without opening her eyes she fumbled for the receiver, answering on the fourth ring.

"Hello?" she said thickly.

She didn't recognize the voice of the male caller who asked for Michael but in the haze of being only half awake, it registered that there was a shower running somewhere nearby.

"Just a minute," she said into the phone anyway, holding her hand over the mouthpiece while she shouted Michael's name.

But there was no response, only the continuing sound of the shower.

So that was the excuse she gave for why Michael couldn't come to the phone. Then she said, "Can I give him a message?"

"Please," the man said. "Tell him Ted called from the station house—"

"Ted," she repeated foggily, still keeping her eyes closed.

"Right. I wanted to let him know that he doesn't have to come in today until about five. He said his arm wasn't bad enough to keep him out, but Frank offered to stay for the first part of his shift so he'd have at least a little break after yesterday."

"Frank—" Josie said, going on to repeat that part of the message, too.

"And, also," the caller said, "would you tell him that we've decided to start a fund to help that family. We all know how it was for Michael losing his dad when he was a kid, and it struck a nerve with us, so we wanted to do something. Anyway, tell him to take it easy today and that we'll see him later."

Josie assured the man she'd give Michael the message and fumbled the receiver back onto the hook without looking. Then she laid back against the pillow and after a few more minutes of really waking up, she opened her eyes.

And that was when it struck her that she wasn't in her own room or her own bed.

She was in Michael's room. In Michael's bed.

After another night of lovemaking with him.

Oh, no, what I have I done?

Josie shot up and swung her legs over the side of the bed, tugging on the top sheet to wrap around herself. Not that the sheet required much force to free it. After three wild rounds, the bedding was all ajumble.

Much like Josie's emotions.

In the cold light of day the rationale that had made mincemeat out of her resolve the night before suddenly seemed a little flawed. Yes, she'd lived in the moment, the way Sharon had encouraged her to. She'd allowed herself to give in to what she'd wanted, what her body craved.

But now the moment had passed. And here she was, in his bed, wondering what she was going to do now.

Not that she didn't know what she wanted to do now, because she did. She wanted to call in sick to work and stay right where she was. She wanted to wait for Michael to get out of the shower, to let him know he didn't have to go in himself until the end of the day, and to spend the next several hours in bed with him.

But what if she did that? What if she went on merely living in the moment? What if she went on surrendering to her own baser instincts and making love with him whenever the urge struck?

Then she'd be living with him, only pretending to be his fiancée, but she'd be intimately involved with him, too.

And it wouldn't be an intimate relationship that had come about the way it should have come about. It wouldn't be an intimate relationship that they'd entered into because they were both ready to take that step. Because they were committed to each other.

It would be an intimate relationship that they'd plunged into because they couldn't control themselves. Because they couldn't keep their hands off each other despite the fact that they were both anti-commitment.

And that was the biggest problem—they *were* both anticommitment. Nothing had changed on that front, had it?

Or had it?

The more Josie considered some of the feelings that were running through her right then, the more it almost seemed as if something *had* changed. For Josie at least.

And that gave her pause.

Had something changed?

It must have. Because far in the recesses of her mind, she realized she was actually imagining herself giving up the fight against getting attached to anyone and becoming more than friends and room-mates with Michael.

More than friends and roommates...

Did she want to be more than friends and room-mates with Michael?

She had to admit that it was tempting. Tempting to just throw everything out the window and say, *Let's go for it.* Tempting to own up to the fact that she had a weak spot where Michael was concerned. That she was more than merely attracted to him.

That she wanted to be with him as much as she possibly could. In any way she possibly could. That she didn't want him to be with anyone else. Ever or in any way. That she wanted to explore every aspect of a relationship with him. Maybe a long-term relationship.

But even as tempted as she was, she was even more terrified.

And she couldn't ignore that.

She was terrified of what might really come of exploring every aspect of a relationship with him. Terrified of opening herself up that much to any man, but worse, to a man who could so easily be taken away from her as randomly, as quickly, as her parents had been.

Besides, what was she going to do? she reasoned. Just wait for him to come back to the bedroom and blurt out that she wanted a relationship with him, after all? And then what?

She doubted that anything was different for him. So what if they'd slept together? Again. It wasn't as if he'd proclaimed his undying love for her, was it? It wasn't as if, in the throes of passion, he'd said he was ready to settle down with her and her alone. It wasn't as if he'd said that making love to her had altered his long-held beliefs and vows to himself. That it had made him want to set an entirely new course for his life.

Which meant that if she was to even broach the subject of being more than mere friends and room-mates she was very likely to face an awful rejection. A hideously painful rejection. A rejection that there would be no bouncing back from.

And no matter how tempted she might be, no matter what she might be imagining, Josie knew she couldn't put herself that far out onto a limb.

So what was she going to do? she asked herself again.

Only this time there seemed to be just one answer.

It was better to reinstate their original agreement. It was the only thing *to* do. Reinstate their original agreement and use the fear of him discovering she might want more and rejecting her because of it, as the impetus to keep herself out of his bed from now on.

That was what she was going to do, she decided. That was what she *had* to do.

And she needed to begin the process by getting out of his room, by getting dressed, by putting distance and decorum between them again before she told him it was back to square one for them.

So Josie got up from the bed and headed for the door.

But she'd barely reached it when the bathroom door opened and Michael came into the bedroom behind her.

"You're up. Good morning," he said.

Josie couldn't very well fling the bedroom door open and run. Even though that was what she wanted to do.

But she also couldn't make herself turn around

to look at him, either. Not and trust that she wouldn't end up in his arms once more.

She just held on tight to her makeshift toga and stared down at the door handle.

''You just had a phone call,'' she told him unceremoniously, relaying the complete message.

For a moment after she was finished Michael didn't say anything at all. Then, in a tone that was much less cheery than the one he'd greeted her with, he said, ''Yesterday. Wow, I'd put that out of my head.''

But clearly thoughts of the day before were in his head now. No doubt reminding him of that family that had lost its father. That family he'd identified with. That family whose grief he was so determined not to wreak on any wife or child of his own. Determined enough to deny himself a wife or child or any close ties as long as he did the job he did...

''I need to get to work,'' Josie said then, hating that it came out sounding so sad, so hurt. Hating that that was how she felt suddenly.

Apparently, Michael heard it in her voice because he said, ''Are you okay?''

''I'm fine,'' Josie lied. She was feeling a lot of things but fine wasn't one of them.

''You don't seem fine,'' he persisted.

Still staring at the door, Josie decided that she couldn't wait for distance or decorum to let him know what she'd decided. That she'd better tell him right then, before they went any further.

So she said, ''Last night was—''

"Incredible."

She'd been going to say that last night had been a mistake. Of course he was right, too. It was just that it was an incredible night that shouldn't have happened and certainly couldn't be repeated. And she was going to have to look him in the eye to tell him that. If for no other reason than to convey how serious she was about what she was saying.

So she finally fired up her courage to turn to face him.

He was standing in the center of the bedroom, wearing nothing but a white towel wrapped around his waist, leaving his sculpted chest and those mile-wide shoulders there in all their glory.

Josie wanted badly to close the few feet that separated them. To slide her arms around him. To press her palms to his naked back, her cheek to his chest. To breathe in the just-washed scent of him. To feel his arms enclose her in their strong splendor.

But she didn't do it. Instead, in keeping with what she'd decided just before he'd come out of the bathroom, she pictured herself doing all that only to have him push her away rather than hold her close. Push her away because she wanted more of him than he was willing to give...

She raised her chin and said, "We broke our agreement."

That put two deep frown lines between Michael's brows. "I guess we did."

"It was an agreement we made for good reasons. Good reasons we *both* had."

"True," he said with a question in his tone, unsure, it seemed, of where she was going with this. Or maybe of where it would end.

"We lost sight of those reasons last night," Josie continued. "But I don't think we should just ignore them now."

Something subtle happened then. So subtle that she wasn't sure if she was imagining it or not. It was as if the Michael who had come out of the bathroom had withdrawn, leaving a more reserved, more contained, less available Michael.

And Josie couldn't help wondering what that meant.

Did it mean that had she said she *didn't* want to go back to their original agreement, he might have said he didn't, either? That maybe he wanted to throw those old reasons out the window, too, to explore the possibility of their having a serious relationship?

But just as she was on the verge of asking those questions, of opening the door on that possibility, Michael said, "You're probably right."

Am I? she wanted to shout.

But she didn't.

What she did do, though, was waver a little. "I mean, we can't have it both ways. We can't be just friends and roommates who have sex—"

"No, I don't suppose we can."

Had she wanted him to disagree? To put up a fight? To say that no, they couldn't be just friends and roommates who had sex, but they could be more than friends and roommates? Was that why every word he said was hitting her like a body blow?

"So," he said, "you just want to go back to the way we started this?"

That was what she'd said. She could hardly deny it now.

Josie merely shrugged. It seemed that with every minute that passed, every word that was said, she was less sure of anything. Less sure of what she wanted. Of what she didn't want. Of what he wanted and didn't want. Of what she might have been able to have if she just hadn't begun this in the first place. If she'd just taken a chance...

"I guess that's what we'll do then," Michael said, interpreting her shrug as confirmation that she wanted to go back to the way they'd started this arrangement. "I promised when we made our deal that it would be on the up-and-up, and I'll do whatever it takes to make sure that's how it is from here on."

Why were there tears in her eyes?

Josie stared at the floor so he wouldn't see the rapid blinking that was keeping them from falling.

"Okay. Good," she said in a scant whisper.

Then, desperate to get out before she actually cried, she said, "I really have to get ready for work."

But before she'd moved, Michael said, "I'm sorry."

He sounded genuinely contrite. As if he believed he'd done something wrong. But he hadn't. She'd wanted to make love with him as much as he had and there was nothing for him to apologize for.

"No... Don't... It isn't..."

But she just didn't know what to say. Or what to do.

In the end she merely spun around, flung the door wide and ran for her own room.

Where she closed the door at the same moment she lost the battle to keep from crying.

For no reason she understood.

"I think that takes care of everything," Eloise said at the end of the staff meeting later that morning. "Unless anyone has anything else they'd like to say."

She paused, scanning the faces of Manhattan Multiples' employees all sitting around the conference table.

The lengthy, expectant silence wasn't the way Eloise usually ended the meetings, and Josie had the sense that her boss wasn't only offering an opportunity for input, that Eloise was fishing for something.

Even when no one spoke up, the founder of Manhattan Multiples said, "No happy news to share with us?" And again Eloise waited, once more looking at them all one by one.

Josie felt the way she had in school when the teacher had asked a question the class should have known the answer to but didn't. Only unlike the teacher, Eloise didn't finally concede and tell them what response she was searching for.

Instead, when she didn't get any response at all, her expression turned disappointed. "All right then. I guess that's it and we should just get back to work."

As the rest of the staff filed out of the conference room Josie gathered the notes she'd taken to type up later, leaving her the last person in the room with Eloise.

"Is it you, Josie?" the other woman asked when they were alone.

After the way the day had begun with Michael, Josie wasn't feeling at the top of her game. She'd had trouble concentrating on the meeting. She felt more down in the dumps than she had since she'd lost her parents. And all she could really think about was Michael and how she might have handled this morning better, what might have come out of it if she had.

So, for a moment, she thought Eloise might be referring to her distraction. But, for the life of her, Josie couldn't figure out how her low spirits had anything to do with Eloise's probe.

"Is what me?" Josie asked.

Eloise got up from the chair at the head of the table, closed the door and returned to sit beside Josie. When she spoke again it was in a confidential tone. "When I came in this morning I went into the staff rest room. There was a pregnancy test in the trash can in there. The cleaning crew had emptied it last night and that's all there was in the can, so it was impossible not to see. A *positive* pregnancy test."

It still took Josie a moment to figure out how Eloise thought that applied to her. "And you're asking if it was mine?"

"It either belongs to one of us or to someone on the cleaning crew," Eloise reasoned. "I thought if it was one of us, with a little encouragement, they might make the announcement at the meeting. But since no one came forward, I'm a little worried this isn't happy news."

"Well, one way or another, it isn't *my* news," Josie assured her.

"Do you have any idea who it is, then? Is anyone you know of showing symptoms or signs? Or can you think who was here late enough last night or early enough this morning to be the one?"

"No, I can't. I didn't pay attention to who was still here when I left last night or who got in before me."

Eloise was looking more concerned the further this conversation went. "It just worries me that for someone to take the test at work instead of home, they might be wanting to hide it. If they're wanting to hide it so they can surprise dad with the news, that's wonderful. But if they're hiding it because they're unhappy about it or something is troubling them, I just want to help."

That was very much like Eloise and Josie appreciated the other woman's compassion and caring even if she wasn't in need of it at that moment.

But all Josie said was, "I'll keep my eyes and ears open. If I get any inkling of who it is, I'll let you know."

Eloise took gentle hold of Josie's forearm. "Thank you. But in the meantime I think I'm going to find a minute or two to talk to everyone—even the cleaning crew—and see if I can't get whoever it is to tell me in private. In case they need our help."

Eloise patted her arm then and left.

Josie finished getting her notes together, thinking as she did about who could be pregnant. Besides Leah, at least. Who could be *newly* pregnant?

But as she was going through a mental checklist of her co-workers, something else suddenly occurred to her. Something about herself.

Hadn't it been quite a while since she'd had a period?

It seemed like it had. *Quite* a while.

Unless she was mistaken.

Maybe it was just due any day and since so much had happened this month it only felt like a lot of time had passed.

She finished piling her papers and notebook on top of each other, picked up her pen and her mug, and then went out to her desk.

She kept her purse locked in her bottom drawer and she unlocked it, rummaging inside her purse for the pocket calendar she kept there. The pocket calendar she marked every month to keep track of her cycles.

But when she opened it to September there was nothing at all noted there. And it was nearly the end of the month.

She flipped back a page to August, finding the date marked with the P that month.

Feeling the beginning of uneasiness, she counted days.

Then she counted weeks.

Then she counted days again just in case she'd made a mistake.

But no matter how she counted or calculated, the result was the same—she should have had a period by now. In fact, she should have had one right about the time she'd moved in with Michael.

And that was twelve days ago.

Twelve days.

Her heart started to pound.

Twelve days.

Could she really be *that* late?

She counted again but of course the numbers stayed the same. And this time she realized that Labor Day weekend would have been right about when she would have ovulated.

Her heart was beating even faster and she felt kind of cold and clammy.

They'd used condoms, she reasoned as if that were enough to alter the count. They'd used condoms every time. Every single time. All weekend.

But abstinence was the only form of birth control that was foolproof—that was a comment made around Manhattan Multiples over and over. Other forms of birth control could fail...

This can't be happening. This can't be happening. This absolutely can't be happening....

It flashed through her mind that maybe she'd

had a period and just forgotten to mark the calendar.

But despite being desperate to believe that, she knew it wasn't true.

Her heart was beating so hard that she thought it might pound right out of her chest.

Pregnant.

Could she really be *pregnant?*

Maybe it was something else. Maybe there was some other reason she'd missed her period. The move, maybe. Or maybe it was just some kind of fluke.

She'd never missed one before, but she'd heard of people who did. And there was always a first time for everything. Maybe she'd just had some hormonal glitch. Maybe it didn't mean anything at all. Maybe she should just call her doctor and go in.

But she knew what would happen if she called her doctor. Her doctor would want to rule out the most logical cause of a missed period. And the most logical cause was pregnancy.

No matter how she looked at the situation, it all came back to the same thing—she could be pregnant.

For a moment Josie felt as if time actually stood still. She wasn't aware of anything around her. Sounds seemed to come from a distance. The surface of her skin tingled. Her stomach did a flip-flop, her head was spinning, and she felt worse than she ever had in her life.

"Josie? Josie?"

Her name being called helped to drag her out of the fog she was in. Partially, at any rate, enough to glance at Leah who was standing beside her, staring at her.

"Are you okay? You look gray," Leah said.

"I'm fine," Josie answered for the second time today without any more truth to it now than there had been earlier with Michael.

Leah didn't look convinced but Josie busied herself putting the calendar back in her purse and relocking the drawer to make it appear that she was getting back to work.

But work was the last thing on her mind and the first chance she had to slip away to the bathroom without Leah noticing, that's what Josie did.

She ran her hands under cold water and when they were icy she pressed them to her cheeks, hoping that would help her gain some control.

What am I going to do? she thought as she stared at herself in the mirror above the sink, searching her own face for some indication that this wasn't what it seemed to be.

There weren't any indications, though. And she knew that the first thing she had to do was to find out if she really was pregnant.

The easiest way to do that was to buy a test and take it.

After talking to Eloise she knew better than to use one from Manhattan Multiples' supplies or to take the test there. But on her way home from work tonight she was going to have to buy one.

And then she was going to have to go home and use it.

Chapter Nine

Josie spent that evening in oblivion. She'd come home from work, done the pregnancy test and rather than wait to read the results, she'd returned to the living room and fallen into a coma-like sleep on the couch.

Yes, she'd had almost no rest the night before because she and Michael had made love three times. And yes, the day had been one of the most stressful she'd ever spent. But sleeping on the sofa had been less a need for rest and more a need for escape. A way to postpone finding out once and for all if she really was pregnant.

Josie didn't know how long she'd been asleep when Pip nudged her awake to let him outside. She only knew the whole house was dark. But she didn't turn on a light. She got up and stumbled through the living room into the kitchen to let the big dog out the back door.

For a moment after she'd closed it behind him she let her forehead fall against the cool glass in the upper half of the door and shut her eyes again.

But try as she might she couldn't maintain her oblivion and she wondered if, upstairs in her bathroom, was proof that she was actually pregnant.

She knew she should probably go up to look at the test. She told herself she should get it over with. But she just couldn't make herself do it.

Instead she pushed away from the door, thinking that maybe she'd be better able to deal with things if she had something to eat first. After all, she hadn't had a single bite of food all day.

With that in mind, she finally flipped on a light. Then, because for some reason the house suddenly seemed too quiet, she also turned on the television set Michael kept on one of the countertops.

The eleven o'clock news was on and as Josie headed for the pantry the anchorwoman announced breaking news in Williamsburg, Brooklyn.

That was the portion of Brooklyn where the brownstone was located and because of that, Josie's interest was piqued. She stopped just short of the pantry and returned to the television as the anchorwoman said there was a fire burning in a Williamsburg apartment building.

When the live shot came onto the screen and the address was given, Josie couldn't help but recognize the area. It was just a few blocks from the brownstone.

A location reporter took over from the anchorwoman then. "We'll be able to show you the fire itself in just a minute," the youthful blond man said. "But first we have the spokesperson for the local fire department on site to answer some questions."

The *local* fire department?

Of course. It only stood to reason. It was just that, until the reporter said that, Josie hadn't put two and two together. Now she thought, Williamsburg. Close to home. Local fire department...

It all added up to *Michael's* fire department...

The camera angle widened to include the spokesperson facing the reporter and in doing that it also brought the row of fire trucks and other firefighters into view behind them.

The spokesperson and the rest of the firefighters in the background were all dressed in the same gear. Some wore fire hats to protect their heads and some didn't, but they were all soiled and soot-stained, and the numbers on the side of the trucks confirmed that they were from Michael's station.

Josie leaned over the counter to get a closer look and turned up the sound.

"What can you tell us about this fire?" the on-site reporter asked.

"We consider it to be under control as of now," the spokesperson answered. "It looks to have started on the second floor and spread rapidly throughout the building. Luckily we've managed to keep it contained to this one structure."

"I understand a firefighter has already been taken to the hospital with injuries."

It was a simple enough statement but it made Josie's heart leap into her throat.

"I'm afraid so," the spokesperson. "One of our men was struck by a burning beam just after we'd evacuated the last of the occupants."

"Who? Who was the firefighter?" Josie demanded, her anxiety level climbing with each passing moment.

But she didn't get an answer. Instead the reporter said, "Can you tell us how he's doing?"

"He was pinned under the beam for a few minutes before two of our other men were able to free him. He was alive but unconscious when they brought him out, and that's all we know at this point. He was taken by ambulance to the hospital."

"But *who* is he?" Josie screamed at the set as anxiety escalated to a powerful rush of panic even greater than what she'd suffered when it had occurred to her that she'd missed her period.

But still there was no mention of the injured firefighter's name.

Just then the angle of the camera altered again and as Josie watched, one of the firefighters in the background removed his hat to wipe sweat from his brow with the back of his hand.

And that was when she recognized Michael.

"He's all right!" she cried out as if there was anyone to hear her.

But it didn't matter that there wasn't. All that mattered was that there, right in front of her eyes, was Michael. Safe and sound. Sitting on the truck's running board, bracing his elbows on his wide-spread knees, dropping his head wearily into his hands.

A surge of relief washed through Josie that was so great she felt almost weakened by it.

He's all right! He's all right! she repeated to herself to soothe the intensity of her reaction.

But somewhere during the process of calming down she began to marvel at just how intense that reaction had been. Intense enough so that, for those few moments, she thought her heart might actually have skipped beats. She knew she'd held her breath. And it had been as if her whole life had hung in the balance.

In fact, her reaction had been so intense that now, in the aftermath, she had to wonder about it.

Yes, Michael was a friend and the possibility of any friend being hurt—or worse—would have caused her stress. But she hadn't felt the kind of stress she would have felt over an endangered friend. She'd felt what she'd felt when she'd heard that her parents had been in an accident. She'd felt worse than when Troy Randall had broken up with her. And in that instant she knew that if Michael had been the injured firefighter she would have been devastated.

Every bit as devastated as if she had a stake in his well-being. A stake higher than that of a friend or a roommate. The kind of stake a real fiancée had…

Apparently one shock hadn't been enough for today. Because it was a shock to realize that none of the preaching she'd done to herself about not becoming attached to Michael, none of the fighting she'd done against her attraction to him, none of her refusals to let things between them take their natural course, had done a single thing. That she very well had just been kidding herself all along to think that she could keep from falling for the guy.

The news report went on to another story and without Michael to watch, Josie turned off the set, leaving herself in the silence of the house again. His house. The house that always felt so empty without him.

And so good when he was there.

And suddenly Josie had even more on her mind than she'd had before.

Had she fallen for Michael? Did she have feelings for him that were already beyond what she'd ever felt for any other man?

For the first time, she considered that. Seriously. Honestly. Evaluating what had been going on with her since the moment she'd met him that night after her poetry reading on the eve of Labor Day weekend.

She'd actually spent three days in bed with him—that should have been her first clue that there was a difference with this man. That was definitely not something she'd ever even considered before.

Not even with Troy whom she'd thought she loved. Three days of absolutely mindless passion that she'd wanted never to end.

And even when it had, even when they'd agreed not to see each other, had Michael been out of her head for so much as one full day during those two weeks that followed?

No, he hadn't been. Every day they were apart she'd found her mind wandering to him, she'd found herself wondering where he was at any given moment, wondering if he was thinking about her, if he was struggling with the desire to call her the way she'd struggled with the desire to call him, if he was lying in bed every night reliving that weekend and craving a rerun the way she was.

And then he'd shown up on her doorstep with his crazy pretend-engagement scheme.

She couldn't deny that it had helped her out with Pip and her housing problem, but she hadn't had to think too long or too hard about it to agree, had she?

And then there was the time since she'd moved in with Michael. Sure, she'd tried to ward off her attraction to him. But had it worked? Hardly. Spending every minute they could together, kissing, finally making love again—none of that had come from nowhere.

Any more than her terror at the thought that he might have been hurt tonight had come from *not* having fallen for him. From *not* having feelings for him that went beyond what she'd ever felt for any other man.

''So, admit it,'' she told herself.

And then she did. She admitted that she did have feelings for Michael. Feelings that had begun to peek out from behind their camouflage this morning. That's why she'd been tempted to suggest they put aside what they'd agreed to and just go for it. That's why she'd been tempted to suggest they be more than friends and roommates, that they explore every aspect of a deeper relationship.

And now, after the scare of thinking he might have been hurt—or worse—the feelings she had for him seemed to have cast aside that camouflage completely and thrust their way to the surface. Where she couldn't pretend they could be kept under control any longer.

Because they couldn't be.

She definitely had feelings for Michael.

For Michael who was in one of the highest risk occupations there was, she reminded herself. For Michael who had already given her a sample of the kind of fear tonight that she'd wanted never to experience again...

''What if he had been the firefighter who was hurt tonight?'' she said out loud, as if that might have a stronger effect against those feelings for him.

But instead of finding support in thoughts of how horrible she would have felt, instead of finding cause to withdraw to protect herself, something else was at the forefront of her mind.

What she was really thinking was that if she had lost Michael tonight, she would have wasted precious time she could have had with him. Precious time during which the only thing she'd really accomplished was to deny herself what she'd wanted.

Because despite everything else, what she wanted now, what she'd wanted since the moment she'd set eyes on him, was Michael.

More than she wanted to protect herself. More than she wanted anything.

"Or maybe I've just lost my mind," she said, wavering in the newness of the realization.

What about her independence? What about not wanting to be tied down? Wanting to go on being a free spirit? she asked herself.

But somehow none of that seemed as important now as it had before, either. It certainly didn't seem as important as Michael did. As important as being with him did.

"So Sharon knew what she was talking about."

Because hadn't Sharon said that when it was the right person, it didn't feel like being tied down or losing freedom?

She had. And now Josie understood it because the idea of being with Michael for an eternity didn't seem at all like being tied down. It seemed like heaven.

Plus, maybe she was grasping at straws, but something else her friend had said suddenly occurred to her.

Sharon had pointed out that the vast majority of people even in high-risk jobs went through their entire careers without anything awful happening to them. And hadn't the news report supported that?

One man had been injured but as the camera had panned the scene, there were any number of other people still working, still fine.

And Michael was one of them.

Michael was the one of them who made everything in her come alive. The one of them who seemed to have gotten into her bloodstream.

Maybe literally...

What came to mind then gave her another reason to pause.

How much of an influence on all this was the possibility that she could be pregnant?

Maybe not too much since this was the first time she'd thought about it since the news came on.

But there was no doubt that if she did prove to be pregnant it would raise the stakes for her.

And that seemed like the best reason yet not to go upstairs to find out for sure.

As long as she didn't know for sure, there was still a part of her that didn't believe it was true. That allowed her the freedom to figure out where she and Michael might be able to go from here without pregnancy being a factor.

And that seemed all the more important to Josie when she remembered what had kept her from acknowledging her feelings this morning.

Just because she felt differently didn't mean Michael did.

Yes, there had been that moment when she'd wondered if things might have turned out differently if she hadn't initiated the return-to-their-original-agreement talk. But she still couldn't be certain about what was going on with Michael. And until she knew that, she didn't think she could bear to add the element of a pregnancy to the picture.

For now, she just needed to know if Michael's feelings had changed. If he wanted her the way she wanted him and for no other reason than because they cared about each other.

For now, she just needed to know if they had a chance....

But she also didn't think she could go the rest of the night until Michael got home in the morning without knowing any of that.

In fact, she didn't think she could go another hour.

"He's only a few blocks away," she reminded herself then.

And that was all it took.

Acting on pure impulse, Josie called for Pip to come back inside, and locked the door.

Then she hurried out of the kitchen and through the living room, jammed her feet into the shoes she'd slipped off to take her nap and nearly ran for the front door.

She didn't start to consider how she looked until she was halfway up the street. So, as she power-walked, she ran her fingers under her eyes in case her mascara had smeared. She pinched her cheeks to substitute for blush. She finger-combed her hair, smoothing it behind her ears. And she tucked her white, V-necked T-shirt into her jeans, hoping it was all enough to make herself at least presentable.

Then she rounded the last corner to get to the block where the fire was and came up short to find herself at the rear of a large crowd of people gathered to watch what was going on up ahead.

But Josie had a goal and she wasn't going to let even a wall of onlookers stop her.

Muttering "Excuse me" over and over again like a chant, she eased herself into every separation in the crowd, forcing herself through, sometimes saying, "I have to get up there," as if it might be her own apartment that was burning.

As she neared the front she spotted Michael still sitting on the fire truck the way she'd seen him on TV and she tried calling his name. But she was too far away for him to hear her and he merely went on talking to another firefighter who had joined him on the running board.

But Josie didn't give up. She continued pushing through the crowd until she finally reached the very front.

Except when she did, she was met by a yellow tape strung up to keep everyone at a distance and several police officers who were enforcing the rule on the other side of that tape.

"I'm sorry, but I have to get closer. I have to speak to one of the firefighters," Josie informed the policewoman standing directly in front of her to block her progression.

"No one is allowed beyond this point," the policewoman answered flatly.

Something about Josie's level of desperation must have alerted another officer working a few feet away because he joined the policewoman to reinforce the dictate and to become a greater obstacle.

"Please," Josie begged. "I won't go anywhere near the fire. I just need to see Michael Dunnigan. He's sitting over there, on the side of that second truck. You can see him from here and I won't go any farther than that. It's important."

"Nobody gets beyond this point," the male officer said, emphatically echoing his female counterpart.

"You don't understand. I *have* to talk to Michael Dunnigan!"

Josie had raised her voice and she wasn't sure if the scene she was causing caught Michael's attention or if saying his name the second time had done the trick, but suddenly he was coming toward her.

"It's okay, let her in," he told the police officers.

They still weren't eager to comply but after another moment they finally did and Josie ducked under the tape.

She met Michael a few feet inside the line.

"What's the matter?" he demanded, sounding alarmed.

They seemed to have become the floorshow by then and since Josie didn't relish having an audience for what she was about to do, she pointed to a spot across the street and behind the fire trucks. "Can we go over there?"

Michael didn't waste any time questioning the

request. He just placed a hand at the small of her back and guided her across the street.

The moment they were out of earshot, though, he said, "Why are you here?"

It was strange, but until that moment she hadn't had a single qualm about this course of action. She hadn't thought about the reality of actually doing what she was doing. Or of where she'd be doing it—in the middle of a fire, of all things, while Michael was working.

But now that she was here, facing him, with so much going on around them, she realized this might not have been the best choice of time or place.

"I'm sorry. This was stupid," she said. "I shouldn't have come here. Now. I wasn't thinking."

"But why did you? Is something wrong?"

It finally registered that he was afraid some kind of emergency had brought her here. But then, what else would he think but that nothing short of a personal emergency could have caused this?

"Nothing's wrong. I know it seems like something should be for me to do this but it's just that I saw the news and they reported that a firefighter was hurt and at first I was afraid it was you, and then I saw you and knew you were okay, but then—"

Michael cut into her rambling. "Slow down, Josie. Is that why you're here? To make sure I'm all right?"

"No," she said rather artlessly.

"Then why?"

For a split second she debated about going through with this. But she was already here. She'd already pulled him away from his work. And if she didn't tell him what she'd come to tell him, she didn't know if she'd ever have the courage again.

"Okay, this was a really dumb thing for me to do right now. It's just that I got so scared that you were the guy who had to be taken to the hospital and then, after I knew it wasn't you, I started to think about just how scared I'd been and... Well, I realized some things. Some things that I'd started to think this morning but chickened out of saying, and I just had to tell you that what I ended up saying this morning wasn't true. I don't want to go back to our original agreement. I want more than that," she ended up blurting.

"You came to tell me that now? I thought something had happened."

Not exactly the response she'd hoped for.

"Something did happen," she went on, anyway, feeling as if she were rolling downhill and couldn't stop herself. "For a minute I thought I might have lost you and I realized that we would have wasted what time we could have had together. I guess I just couldn't waste another minute."

Michael was staring down at her, his brow furrowed into a frown that told her nothing of what he was thinking except maybe that he thought she might have lost her mind.

Then one of the other firefighters shouted to him, "Hey, Mikey, we need to go in again."

"I'll be right there," Michael called back. Then to Josie he said, "I can't talk about this now."

Of course he couldn't, Josie thought, wanting to kick herself. "This was bad. I know. I'm sorry. I'm a little nuts today."

"It's okay," he assured in a soothing voice when he had every right to be aggravated with her instead. "We'll talk when I get off, okay?"

So all of this had been for nothing and she was still going to have to wait until the next morning.

But what could she say?

"Sure. I understand," she nearly whispered through her own disappointment.

The same firefighter who had yelled to Michael before shouted his name again, as if to remind him that he was needed.

Michael answered only with a raising of his chin.

Then to Josie he said, "Come on. I'll have somebody take you home."

She didn't know who that somebody would be, but she knew she didn't want to have to explain to anyone what in the world she was doing. "No, that's all right. I'll just go back myself."

"I don't know, Josie, you're—"

"I'm all right," she assured him in a hurry.

"Dunnigan!" the other man shouted.

"You're sure?" Michael asked.

"Go on," she urged.

He didn't have any other choice, but still he paused long enough to search her face with those green eyes of his, as if to convince himself she genuinely was okay.

"We'll talk when you get home," she said to send him on his way. "Just be careful."

"Always," he answered, but it was obvious he still wasn't certain what to make of her or, maybe, of what she'd just said to him.

He didn't have any choice but to get back to work, though, and she couldn't remain here where onlookers weren't allowed, so she waved him off and returned to the sidelines, almost slinking through the crowd to retrace her steps back to the house.

But the whole way there she just kept thinking that she'd pretty much said what she'd wanted to. That without giving Michael any of the details she'd let him know that she wanted more with him than their original agreement provided for.

And she was all too aware of the fact that he hadn't jumped in and said he did, too.

Chapter Ten

By 2:00 a.m. Michael was back at the fire station, packing his duffel to go home. He'd broken open his stitches at the fire and ended up in the emergency room again with orders to take a few days off until the wound closed.

He hadn't put up a fight. Not only had the arm hurt like hell until it had been shot with lidocaine again, but after Josie's appearance at the fire he had a lot to sort out in his head, too.

Which was also the reason he'd turned down the offer of a ride when he was ready to leave work and instead opted to walk the half mile in the middle of the night.

The cool autumn air felt good as he left the station and he took a couple of deep breaths to clear his lungs of the smoke he'd inhaled earlier.

Then he set off for home. And Josie.

She'd been on his mind nearly every waking hour of every day since he'd met her so it was no surprise that she was there now. It was just that he wasn't sure what to make of her and what she'd said at the fire.

So she hadn't meant what she'd told him about wanting to go back to their original agreement, he thought.

Okay. That hadn't been what he'd wanted, anyway.

But Josie had said she wanted more and he wasn't exactly sure what that meant. More nights like the last one? More weekends like Labor Day?

Michael was in favor of that.

But did Josie want even more than that? That's what he didn't know.

And it had him worried.

What if she wanted the whole shebang? What if she'd changed her mind about not getting involved, about maintaining her freedom, and decided she wanted more than a pretend engagement? That she wanted the real thing? Marriage. Family. All of it. With him.

Had she forgotten what he did for a living? That it was risky? That something could happen to him at any time and she could end up as grief-stricken as she'd been when her parents were killed?

That didn't seem like anything she was likely to lose sight of. But what if she'd decided taking that kind of risk was okay for her? Because even if she had, that didn't mean it had suddenly gotten to be okay with him.

She knew how he felt. He'd told her. She knew what he and his family had gone through when his dad had died. She knew that he was dead-set against getting married or having kids until he retired. Was she willing to just hang around until then? He doubted it.

So what could she be thinking?

That if he'd been the injured firefighter tonight and he was out of the picture, they would have wasted what time they could have had—wasn't that along the lines of what she'd said?

Maybe Josie had been talking to his mother, he thought. Because that had always been his mother's perspective—that in spite of what they'd all suffered when his father had died, it was worth it to have had what time they did have with him.

"I wonder if the family of that man who died in that car yesterday would agree?" Michael muttered to himself.

But for some reason, he started to think about that. About those people who were mourning and if they were wishing they'd never known the man rather than suffering the loss of him now.

If *he* would rather have never known *his* father

at all so he would never have known the pain of losing him.

Maybe it was strange, but in the years since his dad's death, he'd never thought of it that way. And now that he did, Michael actually felt a little ashamed of himself.

He'd loved his father. He had only good memories of the twelve years he'd had with him. Of holidays. Of his father teaching him to fish. Of his father taking him camping. Of his father playing catch with him or tossing the football around. Of his father taking him to the firehouse. Of his father telling him about the birds and bees.

Would he really have been willing to give that up in return for taking away the pain of losing him?

He didn't have to think twice about that. The answer was no, he wouldn't have. Even if he had the choice, he wouldn't trade a single one of those memories, a single one of those moments, to wipe away all the pain, all the hardship, all of what had come after his dad's death.

Yet that was how he'd been living his own life—as if that time with his dad hadn't been worth it.

He definitely wasn't proud of that.

But as he turned the corner onto his street, he was still torn.

He'd based the whole game plan for his future on the negative. On not wanting to put a wife or kids at risk of losing him. And that still felt pretty valid, too. He couldn't shake the thought that it would be irresponsible to bring a wife and kids into his life as long as he did the job he did. The job he loved.

But that was when something else struck him. Something else about that man from the day before. Something even about so many of the people who had been lost in the World Trade Center tragedy.

That man from the day before had had a low risk occupation. A desk job. He'd been a book-keeper. Yet he'd died two blocks from his home.

And while so many of Michael's brother fire-fighters had been lost on 9/11 and reinforced his feelings that his own job was dangerous, even more of the people lost in the Trade Center had gone to jobs that day that had seemed perfectly safe.

What struck Michael then was that the reality of everyone's life was that anything could happen to anyone at any time. Even if the biggest risk they ever took was to get in a car or to go to an office job.

Given that, was he *never* going to have a wife or kids because just living life came with risks? he asked himself. Was he never going to allow him-self that full life he'd accused Josie of deny-ing herself, because of what *could* happen in the future?

Because if that was the case, it occurred to him that he was going to waste his whole damn life. The way he'd already wasted much of the time he'd had with Josie, just as she'd said.

As he climbed the steps to the brownstone he knew that that wasn't the way he wanted to live. That being without Josie wasn't the way he wanted to live. That he wanted a full and complete life. That he wanted it with her. In spite of everything.

He suddenly knew that he couldn't say no to what he knew was right, right now, just because of what *could* happen down the road, to either of them.

For a moment he stayed in the archway with his key in the lock, asking himself if he was sure about this. After all, in the short space of a half mile he'd done a complete turnaround of one of his most strongly held beliefs.

Was it genuine?

Or was he just getting carried away by the woman inside who he didn't seem able to get enough of?

Both, was the conclusion he came to.

The turnaround was genuine because as he went over it in his mind he knew that living a full life was not only what he needed, what he deserved, it was a way of honoring his dad and what his dad had meant to him.

And he was also carried away by Josie. By all she stirred in him. By all she was to him.

Josie, who had been like the lifeline he'd reached out for himself after prying that man from that car.

Josie, who had been the solace he'd craved.

Josie, who was really all he wanted...

Convinced, Michael finally turned the key in the lock, stepped through the open door and flipped on a light.

But then he flipped it off again fast because Josie was curled up on the couch, sleeping.

The flash of light hadn't lasted long enough to disturb her but it did rouse Pip where he was on the floor in front of the sofa. The big dog loped over to greet him as Michael set down his duffel.

"Hi, buddy," he whispered as he scratched Pip behind the ears.

But all the while Michael's gaze was on Josie.

Moonlight shone through the undraped bay window directly on her face and for the first time he considered what it would mean to allow himself the possibility of a future with her.

It would mean more weekends like Labor Day and nights like the last one, for starters, and that alone was a winning argument. But it would also mean more of being with her in every way. More of talking to her, teasing her, confiding in her, sharing the burdens of whatever came their way.

A future with her meant more of her laughter. More of her fun-loving spirit. More of her outlook on life. More of everything about her that he'd been working so damn hard not to want since he'd first laid eyes on her.

And in that moment he hoped that he was right in assuming that she'd conquered her own fears and reservations about getting involved with him.

Because as he stood there watching her sleep, his heart swelled as if it had been suddenly freed.

And he knew that if he was wrong and Josie hadn't been telling him that she'd resolved her own fears and reservations, that she hadn't been telling him that the *more* she wanted was more of a serious relationship, a serious future with him, he wasn't sure he would be able to stand it.

Even though Josie was asleep, she wasn't sleeping soundly and she was half aware of Michael coming in and Pip going to greet him.

So when Michael showed up next to the couch and said a quiet, "Hey," Josie rolled from her side onto her back and opened her eyes into tiny slits.

"Hey," she repeated groggily.

Michael lifted her legs and sat, putting her bare feet in his lap and giving her toes a gentle squeeze that felt like heaven.

"What time is it?" Josie asked, glad he was home but wondering why.

"It's about two-thirty."

"They let you off early?"

"They did," he said, without explaining the reason.

Josie opened her eyes all the way and pushed herself to sit up against the arm of the couch, making sure not to pull her feet away from the massage he'd begun with those big, warm, strong hands.

"What are you doing sleeping down here?" he asked then.

She couldn't very well tell him about the pregnancy test that waited for her in her bathroom, or that she was avoiding knowing the results, so she said, "Upstairs was off limits until I talked to you."

He nodded as if that made sense and Josie hoped it was a good sign that he wasn't being standoffish.

But he also had a very somber expression on his handsome, moon-dusted face and she couldn't help wondering if the foot rub was a way to blunt the blow of the rejection she'd been worrying he might give.

"I'm really sorry about just showing up like that tonight." She apologized again for her rash behavior.

"It's okay. I'm glad you did."

"Really?" Raw hope echoed in her voice and she consciously toned it down. "Why?"

"Because part of what you said got me to looking at things differently."

"Which part of what I said and what things did it make you look at differently?"

He didn't respond to that immediately. He just

went on rubbing her feet, staring at them for a while.

And when he did speak again it wasn't to answer her question. It was to ask one of his own.

"What did you mean when you said you didn't want to go back to the original agreement, after all, that you want more than that?"

So he was going to put her on the spot. Even the massage didn't help keep her anxiety level from raising again at that. But she was the one who had started this tonight, she could hardly back down now.

"I meant that I don't want to be just friends and roommates," she said, feeling as if she were stepping out onto thin ice despite the fact that her answer was still somewhat ambiguous.

"What changed your mind?"

Josie explained the thought process that had brought her to him earlier, including Sharon's observation that being with the right person was a good thing, that it didn't feel like being tied down. And the whole time she talked, Josie kept her fingers crossed that he wouldn't prove true her worst fears. At least her most recent worst fears of rejection.

"So I'm the right guy, huh?" Michael said when she'd finished, smiling a small smile now.

"You must be to have changed my mind after all this time," Josie said matter-of-factly.

"If we aren't going to be friends and roommates, then what will we be?'' he asked, sounding slightly cocky.

She had the sense that he was toying with her a little. But she thought before she went any further she had to know where he stood.

''I don't know what we'll be. You still haven't said if you even want to be more than friends and roommates.''

Michael didn't answer that readily, either. But his expression wasn't overly somber anymore. Instead it had an element of mischief to it.

Then he said, ''Your surprise visit tonight got me to doing some thinking of my own. It did some eye-opening for me.''

''Eye-opening is a good thing.'' At least the way he said it made it sound as if it were a good thing.

He explained the realizations he'd come to himself tonight, letting her see that he felt as if he'd dishonored his father's memory by putting more emphasis on the grief his father's death had caused rather than on the life his father had lived.

He said, ''I never thought I was a negative kind of guy. I know it isn't the kind of guy I want to be. I also know that there's no way anyone can avoid all the negatives, that the best we can do is enjoy the positives and deal with the negatives when they happen.''

''Translation?''

''I don't want to waste any more of the time we can have together, either. I don't want to waste any more time fighting the fact that I've fallen in love with you. That I want you. That I want a future with you.''

Josie felt as if he'd lit a warm glow inside of her and she found herself instantly fighting tears that came from the pure joy of hearing that.

To hide it, though, she tried a little levity. ''Does that mean there might be a chance that the pretend engagement could become the un-pretend engagement?''

Michael laughed. ''More than just a chance. If we're going to talk about wasting time, I think I've wasted enough of it. Now I want to make up for it.''

''With marriage? A family?'' she asked, still blinking back the joyful tears.

''With marriage to you. And a family with you,'' he confirmed.

Josie scooted toward him until her knees were bent high and her rear end butted against his thigh. ''And were you thinking of starting that family soon?''

Michael laughed again, although this time there was an edge of confusion to it. ''Are you in a hurry?''

Josie debated about whether or not to tell him there could be more of a hurry than he knew. About whether or not now was the time to tell him she could already be pregnant. But in the end she wanted everything between them out in the open and so she said, "Actually, I didn't want to know this myself before, but now…"

She stood and took his hand to pull him with her up the stairs and through her dark bedroom to her bathroom.

Once they were there she turned on the light and finally studied the wand she'd used earlier.

"Apparently I am in a hurry," she said.

"Is that what I think it is?" Michael asked.

"What do you think it is?"

"A pregnancy test?"

"That's what it is, all right. And since positives are the theme of the evening…"

"A baby? We're having a baby?"

"It looks like we are," Josie said, sounding as stunned as he did.

"A baby…" Michael marveled.

"Is that okay?"

"It's okay with me," he said as if he was actually warming to the idea.

That helped Josie considerably.

"What about you?" Michael asked. "Is it okay with you?"

She thought about it now that everything between them was settled, now that she knew they had a future together, judging what she did feel.

And she realized that having a baby with Michael, having Michael's baby, was more than okay.

"I know we didn't plan it and condom failure makes for one very big surprise, but the thought of the two of us making a baby is kind of nice, isn't it?'' she said then in a quiet, heartfelt tone.

They were standing side by side at the bathroom sink and Michael turned her to face him, wrapping his arms around her and pulling her close enough to gaze down into her eyes with the warmth of his.

''It's better than nice, it's terrific. It's especially terrific that two fruitcakes like us, who have spent so much time isolating ourselves, find out we'll not only have each other, but a baby, too.''

Josie smiled up at him. ''It is kind of ironic, isn't it?''

Michael rolled his eyes heavenward. ''I think somebody up there was looking out for us and got us what we needed in spite of ourselves.''

''Your dad and my folks?''

''And my mother down here, we can't forget her. Not that she'll let us,'' Michael added with a laugh.

He kissed Josie then. And kissed her again.

And that was all it took to unleash the desire that always seemed to be simmering just beneath the surface in them both. Kisses that lasted through Josie setting the pregnancy test on the counter again. Kisses that lasted through Michael maneuvering them out of the bathroom and all the way to her bed where clothes began to fly off and urgency gained ground.

They didn't even pull down the quilt that covered her mattress. Naked, they lay on Josie's bed as hands began to explore, as mouths clung in passionate hunger, and bodies pressed together as if each sought out its other half.

When neither of them could wait another moment, seeking out their other half was just what they did.

He came into her as smoothly, as perfectly, as if he'd been designed for her alone.

She wrapped her arms and legs around him, taking him fully inside of her.

And they became one, completing each other with a new openness, a new freedom that shed all inhibitions. That truly joined them, body, soul and spirit, and took them to a level that was profoundly deeper than it had ever been before.

Afterward, spent, replete, blissful, Michael rolled onto his back and pulled Josie to lie on her side to rest her head on his chest.

"I love you, Josie Tate," he said into her hair.

"I love you, too, Michael Dunnigan."

"Will you marry me? For real?"

Josie laughed a soft laugh against his bare pectoral. "I will," she said. "I will marry you for real."

He kissed the top of her head, lingering there for a while before he said, "And will you be the mother of my child?"

This time Josie's laugh held more humor than poignancy. "I'd be happy to." Then, recalling something that had barely registered earlier, she said, "Your mother left a message on the answering machine today. She said there's a sale on wedding dresses and she wants to take me to buy one on Saturday."

It was Michael's turn to laugh. "That woman never gives up, does she?"

"That's my impression," Josie agreed.

"Think you can handle her?"

"I think I can." Actually, there was nothing Josie thought she *couldn't* handle if it meant having him in the bargain.

"So, I guess I should go with her," she said then, just beginning to get used to the idea that things had changed.

"You should. And you can tell her she finally won us over to her side and we want to get married right away. *Right away,*" he added, dropping a gentle hand to her still-flat belly.

Then Michael chuckled a little and said, "You don't think having more than one baby at a time is contagious, do you?"

"I understand it is," Josie joked. "And I've been working with someone who's having triplets so you better watch out."

"Three babies? Now that *would* be ironic."

Michael kissed her head again and then settled back. He sighed and Josie could feel his muscles relaxing, his entire body giving way to exhaustion, and she closed her eyes, too.

But she didn't want to drift too quickly to sleep.

She wanted to lie there and savor the feeling of being in Michael's arms, of knowing they would be together, of knowing they would have a baby.

And as she did she was overwhelmed by the sense that this really had all been the work of unseen forces bringing them together despite all the obstacles they'd erected. That this really was a match made in heaven. And that only the best would come of it.

She also couldn't help thinking about how the previous day had begun, about how it had occurred to her that she might be pregnant.

And she could only hope that whoever it was at Manhattan Multiples who had taken that pregnancy test there, would find an ending as happy and as perfect as she had.

* * * * *

*You'll love the fourth book in
Silhouette Special Edition's
exciting continuity,*
MANHATTAN MULTIPLES
PRACTICE MAKES PREGNANT
*By Lois Faye Dyer
Available October 2003
Don't miss it!*

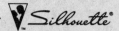

SPECIAL EDITION™

MANHATTAN MULTIPLES
So many babies in the big city!

PRACTICE MAKES PREGNANT

by Lois Faye Dyer

A shy, sweet secretary gives in to desire with a handsome attorney— and ends up with more than she bargained for!

Available October 2003 at your favorite retail outlet.

Visit Silhouette at www.eHarlequin.com

SSEPMP

Visit a new address
in Cedar Cove:

311 Pelican Court

New York Times **bestselling author**

DEBBIE MACOMBER

Rosie Cox
311 Pelican Court
Cedar Cove, Washington

Dear Reader,

Everybody in this town knows that my husband, Zach, and I recently got a divorce. Everybody also knows that the judge decreed a pretty unusual custody arrangement. It won't be the kids moving between my place and Zach's. *We're* the ones who'll be going back and forth!

But the *really* big gossip has to do with the dead guy—the man who died at a local bed-and-breakfast. Who is he? Roy McAfee, our local private investigator, is absolutely determined to find out. I hope he does—and then I'll let you know! See you soon....

Rosie

**"Macomber is known for her honest portrayals
of ordinary women in small-town America, and this
tale cements her position as an icon of the genre."**
—*Publishers Weekly* on *16 Lighthouse Road*

*Available the first week
of September 2003,
wherever paperbacks are sold!*

MIRA®

Visit us at www.mirabooks.com   MDM719

Your opinion is important to us! Please take a few moments to share your thoughts with us about your experiences with Harlequin and Silhouette books. Your comments will be very useful in ensuring that we deliver books you love to read. *Please take a few minutes to complete the questionnaire, then send it to us at the address below.*

Send your completed questionnaires to:
Harlequin/Silhouette Reader Survey, P.O. Box 9046, Buffalo, NY 14269-9046

1. As you may know, there are many different lines under the Harlequin and Silhouette brands. Each of the lines is listed below. Please check the box that most represents your reading habit for each line.

Line	Currently read this line	Do not read this line	Not sure if I read this line
Harlequin American Romance	❏	❏	❏
Harlequin Duets	❏	❏	❏
Harlequin Romance	❏	❏	❏
Harlequin Historicals	❏	❏	❏
Harlequin Superromance	❏	❏	❏
Harlequin Intrigue	❏	❏	❏
Harlequin Presents	❏	❏	❏
Harlequin Temptation	❏	❏	❏
Harlequin Blaze	❏	❏	❏
Silhouette Special Edition	❏	❏	❏
Silhouette Romance	❏	❏	❏
Silhouette Intimate Moments	❏	❏	❏
Silhouette Desire	❏	❏	❏

2. Which of the following best describes why you bought *this book?* One answer only, please.

the picture on the cover	❏	the title	❏
the author	❏	the line is one I read often	❏
part of a miniseries	❏	saw an ad in another book	❏
saw an ad in a magazine/newsletter	❏	a friend told me about it	❏
I borrowed/was given this book	❏	other: _____	❏

3. Where did you buy *this book?* One answer only, please.

at Barnes & Noble	❏	at a grocery store	❏
at Waldenbooks	❏	at a drugstore	❏
at Borders	❏	on eHarlequin.com Web site	❏
at another bookstore	❏	from another Web site	❏
at Wal-Mart	❏	Harlequin/Silhouette Reader	❏
at Target	❏	Service/through the mail	
at Kmart	❏	used books from anywhere	❏
at another department store or mass merchandiser	❏	I borrowed/was given this book	❏

4. On average, how many Harlequin and Silhouette books do you buy at one time?

I buy _____ books at one time	❏
I rarely buy a book	❏

MRQ403SSE-1A

5. How many times per month do you shop for any *Harlequin and/or Silhouette* books?
   One answer only, please.

1 or more times a week	❏	a few times per year	❏
1 to 3 times per month	❏	less often than once a year	❏
1 to 2 times every 3 months	❏	never	❏

6. When you think of your ideal heroine, which *one* statement describes her the best?
   One answer only, please.

She's a woman who is strong-willed	❏	She's a desirable woman	❏
She's a woman who is needed by others	❏	She's a powerful woman	❏
She's a woman who is taken care of	❏	She's a passionate woman	❏
She's an adventurous woman	❏	She's a sensitive woman	❏

7. The following statements describe types or genres of books that you may be
   interested in reading. Pick *up to 2 types* of books that you are most interested in.

I like to read about truly romantic relationships	❏
I like to read stories that are sexy romances	❏
I like to read romantic comedies	❏
I like to read a romantic mystery/suspense	❏
I like to read about romantic adventures	❏
I like to read romance stories that involve family	❏
I like to read about a romance in times or places that I have never seen	❏
Other: _____	❏

*The following questions help us to group your answers with those readers who are
similar to you. Your answers will remain confidential.*

8. Please record your year of birth below.

   19 ____

9. What is your marital status?

   single ❏   married ❏   common-law ❏   widowed ❏
   divorced/separated ❏

10. Do you have children 18 years of age or younger currently living at home?

   yes ❏   no ❏

11. Which of the following best describes your employment status?

   employed full-time or part-time ❏   homemaker ❏   student ❏
   retired ❏   unemployed ❏

12. Do you have access to the Internet from either home or work?

   yes ❏   no ❏

13. Have you ever visited eHarlequin.com?

   yes ❏   no ❏

14. What state do you live in?

   _____

15. Are you a member of Harlequin/Silhouette Reader Service?

   yes ❏   Account # _____   no ❏   MRQ403SSE-1B

eHARLEQUIN.com

Your favorite authors are just a click away
at www.eHarlequin.com!

- Take our **Sister Author Quiz** and
  we'll match you up with the author
  most like you!

- Choose from over 500
  author **profiles!**

- Chat with your favorite authors
  on our **message boards.**

- Are you an author in the making?
  Get advice from published authors
  in **The Inside Scoop!**

- Get the latest on **author appearances**
  and tours!

 *Want to know more about your
favorite romance authors?*

Choose from over 500 author profiles!

**Learn about your favorite authors
in a fun, interactive setting—
visit www.eHarlequin.com today!**

INTAUTH

If you enjoyed what you just read,
then we've got an offer you can't resist!

Take 2 bestselling love stories FREE!

Plus get a FREE surprise gift!

Clip this page and mail it to Silhouette Reader Service™

IN U.S.A.	IN CANADA
3010 Walden Ave.	P.O. Box 609
P.O. Box 1867	Fort Erie, Ontario
Buffalo, N.Y. 14240-1867	L2A 5X3

YES! Please send me 2 free Silhouette Special Edition® novels and my free surprise gift. After receiving them, if I don't wish to receive anymore, I can return the shipping statement marked cancel. If I don't cancel, I will receive 6 brand-new novels every month, before they're available in stores! In the U.S.A., bill me at the bargain price of $3.99 plus 25¢ shipping and handling per book and applicable sales tax, if any*. In Canada, bill me at the bargain price of $4.74 plus 25¢ shipping and handling per book and applicable taxes**. That's the complete price and a savings of at least 10% off the cover prices—what a great deal! I understand that accepting the 2 free books and gift places me under no obligation ever to buy any books. I can always return a shipment and cancel at any time. Even if I never buy another book from Silhouette, the 2 free books and gift are mine to keep forever.

235 SDN DNUR
335 SDN DNUS

Name	(PLEASE PRINT)	
Address	Apt.#	
City	State/Prov.	Zip/Postal Code

* Terms and prices subject to change without notice. Sales tax applicable in N.Y.
** Canadian residents will be charged applicable provincial taxes and GST.
All orders subject to approval. Offer limited to one per household and not valid to current Silhouette Special Edition® subscribers.
® are registered trademarks of Harlequin Books S.A., used under license.

SPED02   ©1998 Harlequin Enterprises Limited